I0675535

First published in United Kingdom in 2025

ISBN 9781036915957

British Library Cataloguing-in-Publication Data:

A catalogue record for this book is available from the British Library.

This book is dedicated to my family for their support throughout my life and to my colleagues who made the ultimate sacrifice.

# Author's Note

During my career as a Scenes of Crime Officer/Crime Scene Investigator, in Northern Ireland, I have examined thousands of crime scenes and, sadly, witnessed extreme suffering.
It is not my intention to open old wounds or to expose the identity of anyone with which I have worked.
These are my personal views and experiences in life, both before, during and post my career as a SOCO/CSI.

It is an insight into how events have brought me extreme emotional highs and extreme emotional lows.

As time passes, more information is floating to the surface, uncovering the extraordinary lengths some people went to, to further their own agendas. My job was to turn over the stones, to look for evidence; not to see what agenda was hiding below.

I dealt with some deeply depraved individuals, whose humanity, if they deserved that term, existed only within their peer groups — and sometimes not even there.

Who or what turns a child, who was sent to school with a jam piece, into a taker of lives? That is a question that should haunt us all.

# Preface

## Who wants to be a CSI?

Is it your ambition to become a Crime Scene Investigator?

Do you feel that you could go the distance?

What do you need in your arsenal to succeed?

There are many questions to consider before you put that application in the post. What you need, to become a CSI, goes far beyond putting on the crime scene outfit that would give children nightmares.

Passing all the courses and obtaining the necessary academic qualifications does not make you a CSI. Well, your name is on the certificates, but that is all. It takes time and experience to hone your crime scene investigation skills.

However, if you do not have excellent social skills and a good coping strategy, your journey along this career pathway will be a short one. Some crime scenes will push you to the limit of your physical and psychological capabilities.

(I have left my desk, for a moment, to go to my safe place, so please excuse me while I compose myself, as committing some of my crime scene experiences to print will not be an easy exercise. It has taken twenty minutes to lock away my historical demons.)

You will encounter horrific crime scenes, many of them, so you must have the ability to maintain your composure. There is no loss of face if you need a moment of solitude before returning to carry on with your examination.

All your emotions will be in play, and they will not stay obediently quiet; if 'the computer says no' and you do not take the hint and withdraw, to reboot, you could find yourself in freefall without a parachute.

Trauma is like a weapon with stealth capabilities, a time bomb; it will drop its payload on your head when you least expect it. The scout movement got it right when they choose the motto 'Be Prepared.'

Well, you are probably thinking, I have painted a picture of doom and gloom; why would I want that? But the rewards for a job well done will give you hope that you can make a difference.

You will experience great elation and pride, especially when the evidence that you discovered leads to an arrest and successful prosecution.

So, if you believe that you can walk the walk, talk the talk, and wear the scary outfit (sorry, kids), do not hesitate; get that application posted and Good Luck!

Book Title: Who wants to be a CSI

Author: Ray Montgomery

## Table of Contents

## Chapter5

## Chapter 6

## Chapter 7

## Chapter 8

## Chapter 9

## Chapter 10

## Chapter 11

## End Note..............................................328

# Chapter 1

## I Hit the Ground Running

I regard myself as being one of life's fortunate people. I was born with asthma, a respiratory condition which, as you know, can prove fatal without constant care. My asthma regime was strictly administered and monitored by my mum, as she was a nurse. I could not have been in better hands.

Nonetheless, my early years were plagued with asthma attacks and daily medication. Thankfully, I was released from its grip at the tender age of eleven years, though it returned to plague me once more some forty years later.

Fast forward to 1986; that was an eventful year. I was diagnosed with kidney cancer. I had no idea that I had this disease until I suffered a crippling pain on my right side; after examination and a biopsy, I was told that I had a cyst on my right kidney.

The examination was completed within two hours of attending hospital. I was given a local anaesthetic and then a long, thin, flexible tube called a catheter was inserted into a blood vessel in my groin. I was able to see images of my insides, on a bank of monitors, and the doctor pointed out a bulge on my right kidney.

The next procedure was more painful. I turned face down and a nurse put pressure on my groin; I brought my knees towards my chest and tucked my head in, forming an arch. I remember the doctor asking another nurse for the '16-gauge' needle he needed to perform a biopsy; that did not sound good. The doctor told me to stay still for a few seconds and it would all be over. He was true to his word: needle in, sample taken, needle out.

Well, you would expect a reward after a performance like that, but no; not even a sticker or a lolly for me. How disappointing. But what was not disappointing was the speedy and exceptional care I received in the old City Hospital, in Belfast.

The cyst was benign, but it had still done some damage; the surgeon needed to remove half of my right kidney. Things moved fast; the operation took place the following day, leaving me with one and a half kidneys. Lucky me.

The next morning the surgeon came to my room and explained what he had done, and that the operation had been a success. I was well pleased; what a result. However, as I was about to find out, this was just the calm before the storm. Pathology tests carried out on the kidney showed that a malignant and aggressive cancer was present.

I was told that the cancer had penetrated the fatty tissue which surrounds the adrenal gland, but no further. The other half of my kidney needed to be removed. On hearing this I told all those present to leave the room for a few minutes; I needed to be alone. I resigned myself to fate and left myself in medical hands. The surgeon removed the other half of my right kidney the next day, as a precaution.

At this time, my dad was terminally ill with lung cancer. The surgeons had considered removing his right lung but concluded that his left lung, which was cancer free, would not sustain him, due to damage from smoking.

So here I was sitting on a hospital bed and receiving morphine for my pain. However, the main thing on my mind was how I was going to tell my parents, and particularly my dad, that I had cancer too. My mum came to visit me often

3

during the early days of my recovery and, one afternoon, as promised, she arrived with my dad, who was wheelchair bound. It is not easy to describe the emotions in that stark hospital room. We wanted to hug each other but the best we could do was hold hands at the side of the bed.

I took a deep breath and broke the news. During one of her visits, I had told my mum that a cyst was the cause of my condition, a harmless lie. Now it was time for the truth, the whole truth and nothing but the truth — along with a little dark humour, of course. I told my dad that I would be in heaven before him. He grinned and told me that he would be the winner of that race. Sadly, time proved him right.

One cold, clammy November evening, my dad asked me to lift him out of bed and place him in his rocking chair, which stood in the corner of his bedroom. I was hesitant; it was difficult not to cause him more pain when I held him. But he just wanted to sit in his chair for a few minutes; afterwards, I gently placed him back in bed. He knew then that it was time to let go of the turmoil and bustle of his mortal life. Holding his hand, I asked him about his pain, and he replied, "It is bad, but Jesus suffered more; now call your mum, please." My mum took care of all his needs, right to the end.

Those words he spoke to me, in the extreme of his pain, have echoed throughout my life; they have provided me with strength and solace during times when I desperately needed his spirit and wisdom to overcome stressful moments in my life. I had lost my North Star. He was fifty-eight.

My cancer had been hiding, like an assassin in the dark, waiting to strike a fatal blow. It failed, unlike those human assassins who murdered many of my colleagues, the armed forces, and too many innocent people on the streets of my country. Murder is the worst of all crimes; it reverberates, like ripples in a murky pond, and stretches out its tentacles to impact the lives of people everywhere.

During one of my follow-up examinations the surgeon explained that the cyst had caused my pain but in doing so it had saved my life.

So, there you have it. I must thank my friend the cyst for saving my life, though I like to leave a bit of room for divine intervention as well.
Yes, I really am one of life's fortunate people.

When I was a young child, I had three dressing up outfits; when I wore them my imagination allowed me to become a police officer, a cowboy, or a spaceman.

The cowboy outfit came with two cap firing guns, one of which I wore with my policeman's outfit because, as all you firearms experts out there know, a spaceman did not have a cap firing gun, he had a laser gun.

I remember the smell and smoke produced as I fired off the reel of paper caps from my toy Colt 45. Great times. I was to inhale an entirely different explosive smell later in life.

My spaceman outfit was eventually complete when, one December morning, a laser gun mysteriously appeared at the bottom of my bed. The innocence of youth.

I searched through old photographs but there was not one of
me dressed in any of my favourite outfits; but here is one
with me dressed as a farmer. Well, I thought I was a farmer. I
am the one front right (sorry, dad joke). If you look closely,
you can see my dog chariot at the rear right of the photo,
parked behind the horse. My dad made this for me using a
tea chest and the wheels from a pram.

I always wanted to be a police officer, and in 1972 I sat an examination at Police Headquarters, Belfast, in the hope of becoming an RUC Cadet. Some weeks later a letter arrived informing me that I had passed the examination, and that I had been chosen, one of four candidates, to attend Hendon Police College, London. Hendon here I come! I thought triumphantly. But this was sadly not to be.

The police required me to sit my O-Levels at Hendon, but my mother wanted me to sit them in Ballyclare High School, so she informed them that I would not be pursuing a career in the police. I was disappointed, of course, but a few years later I realised that she was only being protective; she did not want me to enter an environment where my life could be threatened. I still love her and always will.

I attended Ballyclare High School until the summer of 1974. I have fond memories of my school years; once my asthma had gone, I could play rugby and cricket.

My old connection with Ballyclare High was renewed some thirty-four years later; it was the setting for a Cold Case review that I carried out (the full account of this case can be read in Chapter 2).

When I left school, I embarked on a career with a Belfast bakery company and, at the ripe old age of twenty-two, I supplemented my monthly income by lecturing, in the College of Business Studies, to students attending night class. In fact, the Belfast Education and Library Board paid me a better hourly rate than my employer. Sadly, the building known as 'The College of Knowledge' was demolished recently.

I enjoyed being a guest lecturer so much that I decided to go back to my education, so I travelled over to London to study. It was during my time in London that my father was diagnosed with cancer, so I came home as often as I could. During one trip home my father handed me the Belfast Telegraph, which was open at a page on which the RUC were advertising for recruits.

My father was quietly signalling to me that this was an opportunity to apply for a job that I always wanted to do. When he saw my interest, he whispered in a conspiratorial way, "Don't mention it to your mother, for the time being."

This little exchange had the desired effect. I am sure my father knew that I would apply and of course I did. Some weeks later I attended an interview and medical examination at the Garnerville RUC complex in Belfast. (Garnerville is now the police training complex.)

The medical examination was conducted in a small room next to the interview room, where a doctor measured my height and weight, followed by an examination that I was not expecting. I will not describe this examination in detail other than to say I was at one point asked to cough. Oh, and the final test was for colour blindness.

Having passed the medical, I took a seat in the corridor beside others to await my fate. I was already feeling lucky; some candidates did not get as far as the seats. Maybe it was the cough. My name was called and so I gathered myself and put my best foot forward. With pulse racing, breathing under control and body language positive I gave the regulation knocks and opened the door.

The interview panel consisted of senior officers, and I hoped that my interview preparation would be good enough to see me through.

The first question revolved around my 1972 application to join the RUC cadets. There were some more questions, which had nothing to do with policing and the interview ended.

Several weeks later I found myself in a queue for the barber's shop, this establishment being inside the Training Depot in Enniskillen. I pointed out to the instructor that I had had a haircut before arriving. He was a former Irish Guardsman, and he replied in his best parade ground voice, "That is not a haircut! You will get a proper haircut now."

Ah well, I suppose the barber had to make a living, so the money was well spent. The short back and sides (and then some) cost me the grand sum of fifty pence. If much more had been removed, I would only have needed a chamois leather cloth to buff my pate. I was too young to take shampoo off my shopping list.

It turned out that three other colleagues and I lived quite near each other. It took two hours to drive from my home to Enniskillen, so we organised a round of car sharing during our first few days of captivity. We would leave Enniskillen on a Friday afternoon and return late Sunday night.

'The Depot' was the cauldron where camaraderie and dark humour were forged. These two attributes would turn out to be the superglue that helped stick us back together during times of extreme adversity and loss.

Initial training completed, we left Enniskillen to serve our communities and to fight an ongoing war against terrorism and crime.

Wearing a police uniform for the first time brought back memories of my time running around the farmyard in the police outfit that Santa had brought me. But that memory soon faded; this was most certainly not a game.

Having served my two-year probation period, which included yet more exams, weapons training, advanced driving skills and fitness training, my growing ambition was to become a Scenes of Crime Officer (SOCO).

Several years passed with no vacancy in sight but, in July 1990, after I had successfully completed a Scenes of Crime course the previous year, I was transferred from Castlereagh RUC Station, Belfast, to the Scenes of Crime office based in

Tennent Street RUC Station. I walked into the SOCO office, around seven that Monday morning, and introduced myself.

Jim, who ran the office, showed me to my desk, shook my hand and, looking at me over the top rim of his glasses, said, "Welcome to the mad house, cub." Well, cub was better than son, I suppose.

I had first encountered trauma at an early age, but I had no concept of what it was. I was only doing what my father asked me to do. I was six years old. My father handed me a cardboard box and told me to recover my dead pup from the top field, as it had been killed by the reaper. Did this task act as a flashbulb moment, summoning in the beginning of the end of my childhood.

Imagine the fallout if you were to ask a six-year-old child, today, to recover their dead pet. Perhaps my father believed that I was ready to cope with such an ordeal. I can still recall the image today. The remains of the poor little creature were held together by the skin along the length of its back.

But back to the SOCO office in Tennent Street. There was no rank structure within SOCO at that time; the senior man ran the show; and what a show it turned out to be. I was detailed to accompany a SOCO to crime scenes for four weeks, as an observer; a kind of honeymoon period. We were about to leave the office, job list in hand, when several office phones rang.

Well, the honeymoon period ended abruptly right then; it had lasted less than two hours. There had been an RPG 7 rocket attack on Grosvenor Road RUC Station, and I was asked to attend Castlereagh RUC Station, to carry out a forensic examination of a prisoner suspected of having been involved in the incident. I was in the thick of battle straight away.

Such an examination is precise, intricate, up close, and personal. Let me give you an idea of what takes place in a nine foot by nine-foot decontaminated room. There is a table and two chairs, a ceiling light, me, and the suspect. Some suspects choose to stand while others prefer to sit, when given the choice.

The reason for this examination is to link the suspect to the scene through explosive residues, DNA, fibres, and head hair. The suspect could have fired the RPG 7, or he could have been in a property during the planning stage of the operation.

I start by reading a document (it is a legal requirement) to the suspect explaining the procedure and what potential evidence I need from him, and that I require his written consent to obtain the samples. Almost all suspects decline to sign the consent form. I then inform him that I have the legal right to obtain the samples without his consent and I sign and date the form, acknowledging non-consent.

The explosive and firearms test kit contains all the equipment that I need to carry out my examination; white coverall, sealed wet swabs, several pairs of clear gloves, nail scraping kit, comb embedded with cotton wool and nylon bags. Having opened the kit, I suit and glove up. I swab the surfaces of my own gloves. So why do I swab my gloves? This is a control sample, which a scientist will later examine for contamination. If contamination is found, then the contents of the entire kit is of no evidential value.

I then swab the suspect, take nail scrapings, head hair combing and swabs containing his saliva. I change gloves after each procedure and all swabs and other samples are sealed individually and placed in a container which I seal, sign, date and submit, as soon as possible, to the forensic science laboratory for examination. The areas of interest for swabbing are his hands, face, and hair. These are the main areas, on the body, where explosive residues accumulate.

The final part of my examination is to have the suspect remove his clothing and footwear, which I package, individually, into nylon bags, seal, and then I attach my evidence labels. Nylon bags are used as they do not absorb explosive residues. Most suspects drop their own clothing into the bag while I hold it open.

However, some would take their clothing off and throw it across the room. I suppose they saw that as their personal protest, against authority. As a suspect was being escorted from my presence, I always thanked him, face to face, for his cooperation.
On a few occasions my politeness was met with a violent outburst of rudeness and pent-up aggression. I constantly talked during such examinations, so perhaps some suspects regarded this as a form of mental torture, and when the opportunity arose, they verbally exploded.

Oh! And the suspect does not leave my presence naked. He is given a white boiler suit and white plimsoles to wear. All sizes and shapes were catered for.

The forensic scientists who examine the contents of the swab kit and the suspect's clothing are looking for explosive residues left behind after the RPG 7 has been fired. They also examine the clothing to see if it sheds fibres; then if fibres are submitted from the scene, they can compare them to link a suspect to the scene through trace contact. The suspect's mouth swabs, contained within the swab kit, are examined and a DNA profile is obtained.

The good news was that no one was killed or severely injured, because of this terrorist attack.

This was still a baptism of fire, though. I had indeed hit the ground running. The four-week observation period was never resurrected.

Most of my police service was spent as a SOCO/CSI in greater Belfast, with short deployments in Newtownards and Maydown, Londonderry (or Derry, for those who prefer this place name).

I have always had and still maintain an impartial view on many topics. I joined the force to uphold the rule of law, to the best of my ability, and I have a proven record to support this. A criminal is a criminal regardless of their background and beliefs.

Do I miss the job? Only sometimes. Do I miss the camaraderie? Well, the simple answer to that is yes. My role as a SOCO/CSI has humbled me on many occasions and psychologically brought me to my knees, as I dealt with the devastation laid bare in front of me.

The primary role of a SOCO/CSI is to carry out a forensic and or fingerprint examination of a crime scene to recover potential evidence. However, there have been many scenes where I have needed to call on my social skills. Traumatic crime scenes can humble you, while simultaneously extracting your physical and mental energy. Memories of such incidents remain with me like limpets stuck to a rock; not even a tsunami could release their muscular grip. A common phrase comes to mind that describes it best: what is seen cannot be unseen.

In Shakespeare's play, *The Merchant of Venice*, Shylock wanted to remove a pound of flesh from Antonio. As a Scenes of Crime Officer/CSI, metaphorically speaking, I lost numerous pounds of flesh over the years and there was no Portia to come to the rescue; there were only the twins 'Dark Humour' and 'Alcoholic Beverage' to numb the senses.

I lived through many dark times, made even darker for some by Alcoholic Beverage.

There was no sign of Duty of Care or Duty to Treat charging over the horizon to provide support, like the 18th Light Dragoons did at Waterloo when they charged the French lines.

So, do I suffer from PTSD? Of course, I do. Do I control my PTSD? Not always. I take daily medication which boosts my serotonin levels. Some refer to this medication as 'the happy pill.' We have the late writer Aldous Huxley to thank for this terminology.

Would I have swapped being a SOCO/CSI to avoid having been diagnosed with PTSD? Never, because I believe what I achieved, as a SOCO/CSI, made a difference.

Enter Hollywood, stage left or right as you prefer.

I do not remember who it was but some officer with elevated rank and too much time on his hands, assisted by some assiduous civil servant, made the executive decision to change the name of our service from SOCO to CSI around 2003.

I have good recall, but such an event never made it into my memory bank.
What I am sure of is that those who decided on this name change probably had Sky television and were ardent fans of CSI Miami, CSI Las Vegas, or CSI New York, or perhaps all three.

On a personal note, I liked CSI Miami but if I am honest, I cannot see *CSI Belfast* making the big screen anytime soon. However, that did not stop me wearing a pair of (non-service issue) shades, for a while, to at least look the part, just in case a Hollywood scout was passing and needed a stand-in.

Truth be told I saw the name change as another erosion of the footprint that the acronym SOCO stood for and what those who served in this unit brought to the table. In fairness,

I realise that change in all levels of society is inevitable, but it is not always for the good.

'The Troubles' is an old term, used many times in the past and it was resurrected, once more, to describe what took place in Northern Ireland over more recent decades. This two-word term, for me, is like describing the French Revolution as a breach of the peace that got a little bit out of control.

We, and by 'we,' I mean the RUC and combined security forces fought a war and nothing short of a war. This war was all encompassing, and it dragged in many people, and many professions, along the way. And there is another thing; using the term 'The Troubles' to describe the events of those years conveniently buried another two-word term: war pension.

While I am on my soapbox, ranting about words, I have an issue with the word closure.

Who gets closure in life? If you have a loved one who has been killed, because of a criminal act, that wound will always be open. If you have a child whose life has been cut short, how can closure be attained? I put the word closure, in these circumstances, in the same category as mermaids and unicorns. In other words, it does not exist in my world. But it may exist in yours.

In these circumstances it is time that wears the crown. As time passes, we can cope better, until someone or something brings the trauma to the fore once more.

Time is also the enemy of those innocent people, and I stress the word 'innocent,' who are part of the legacy issues, as it grinds away, taking the hope for justice and settlement with it.

The last three years of my service were spent in the CSI unit, at Ballynafeigh RUC station, Belfast. This area has fond memories for me as this is where I began my police service, as a beat officer on the Ormeau Road. So, in the end I finished my police career right where I had started it.

During my pre-retirement week, in 2007, I took the time to call at various police stations and say my farewells to those police officers and Crime Scene Investigators whom I admired for their skills and dedication. I had a soft spot for, and especially admired, those who were unpolished in dealing with their workloads.

I was sitting at my desk in Ballynafeigh, with one more day to go before retiring, when a colleague walked in and told me that he had organised a farewell function for me, at a well-known County Down golf club.

Before I could respond he informed me that I would be going, end of story.
I arrived at the function, along with my family and friends, but I could not find a parking space near the clubhouse, so I dropped the crust grabbers, along with the boss, at the front door and drove off to park.

While circling the car park I scanned the golf course and noticed that very few golfers were playing. This was my last chance to do a runner! Having parked the car, I entered the club house, and a wave of emotion took hold, as I took in the large crowd in front of me. I sucked in a deep breath and remembered a saying my daughters use: 'grow a set;' so, I did.

After handshakes, hugs, and kisses we dined. And I have to say, there were some lingering hugs and whispers in my ear that humbled me for a second time in a matter of minutes.

I was still absorbing the moment as I fed my face. When I stood up to reply to those who had spoken about me, as a person and an officer, I took a few seconds to absorb what had been said and to scan the room. I noticed others walking into the room, so I waited until everyone had entered before speaking. I thanked everyone for coming, wished them a pleasant journey home and hoped they had enjoyed their meal.

Someone shouted, 'You're not getting away that light!' So, I continued. The festivities went on for several hours. On my way to the car, gifts in hand, I inwardly reflected on the day. What a fantastic farewell!

At this time, my thoughts drifted back to those of my colleagues who never made it this far, due to the savagery of others, and to my squad mates on the Wall of Remembrance.

Having retired in 2007 I was looking forward to time away from the coalface. However, I was just six weeks into my retirement when I was offered a job by my old employers.

The task was to visit every police station in Northern Ireland and record the amount of evidence that was stored at each location, and then submit a report based upon what I had found. The aim of the exercise was to store all the items under one roof.

My visit to Clogher police station brought back a fond memory. I was never stationed in Clogher but while I was at Musgrave Park Hospital, Belfast, recovering from spinal surgery, I met Eustace, a farmer and part-time officer in the Ulster Defence Regiment. We were both recovering in the same ward. I listened intently as he recalled his close encounter with death.

Eustace had been ambushed, while on his farm, by the Provisional IRA, but managed to escape, though badly wounded. He was able to push through and jump over hedges, mostly due to the adrenalin coursing through his body and the will to live. As a result of this cowardly attack, he sustained permanent nerve and muscle damage. He showed me his wounds; there were thirteen of them. Unlucky for some.

Eustace and I had some laughs as we tried to outdo each other during our daily sessions of water physiotherapy. Our jovial moments helped us battle the pain of recovery. So, while I was searching Clogher police station I asked the station Sergeant if he knew Eustace; he did. He told me that Eustace was a well-known and respected member of the community and that he had sadly passed away recently. For me Eustace was one of life's gentlemen and I feel the richer for having spent time in his presence back in 1981.

This short-term contract lasted three months and then it was back to retirement.

The summer of 2007 was beckoning when I took a phone call from a person who introduced himself as Al. Our paths had never crossed but I had attended crime scenes in the division where he had been stationed.

He informed me that I had been highly recommended and asked if I would be interested in joining a new investigation team, as its forensic reviewer. I was intrigued by this offer and so I agreed to a meeting.

Al arranged a meeting between me and the serving police officer who was to head this new unit. The meeting was very casual, but between us we struck a deal with regards to my hourly rate. This was a first for me. A senior officer was asking me to tell him what I considered a fair hourly rate for my services. He clearly had a budget. When I suggested a rate he agreed, faster than a stooping falcon, followed instantly by a smile. I thought that I was a good poker player, but he must have noticed a tell. Well anyway, I made him happy, and I was pleased with the outcome.

On 2nd July 2007, I joined the Retrospective Murder Review Unit (RMRU), based in Seapark. My role in RMRU was to carry out a review of the forensic evidence in unsolved murder cases and submit my findings to the SIO within RMRU.

Selecting cases for review was the responsibility of a serving PSNI officer, with whom I had several frank (that is, heated) discussions, during my tenure, to forensically progress some cases. There was one case where I vehemently disagreed, albeit in an adult and constructive manner, with this person's investigative — or lack of — knowledge surrounding the case.

My opinion on how to progress the case was dismissed and summarily kicked into touch without an explanation.

When I returned to my desk, I had a new email. It was from my verbal sparring partner, informing me that I was not to attend future senior management meetings. I was to deliver any forensic opportunities via a Detective Sergeant, who in turn would deliver my findings to the Senior Management Team. I thought to myself, good luck with that. The SMT were all serving police officers; two chief inspectors, one detective inspector, two detective sergeants and of course myself, before I was kicked into the long grass.

Prior to the next SMT meeting I complied with the requirements my 'colleague' had imposed. My baby, as it were, was still in the bath water. A little later that morning the SMT sent a runner to find me, as they could not reach me via the phone. They needed my personal input once again. I obliged (there is no I in team). However, I was still barred from the SMT. They had a different interpretation of what constituted teamwork. Well, 'to each their own.' This format endured (or rather, I endured it) until my services were no longer required.

During my retirement I also had the opportunity to pass on my crime scene investigation knowledge to the Turkish Gendarmerie, based in Ankara and the Jordanian Police, based in Amman. What an opportunity and experience that was; but that is a story for another day. However, what I will tell you is that comparing the mind-set of a Gendarmerie officer, a Jordanian officer and myself, with respect to investigating crime, we were all singing of the same hymn sheet. It was a privilege to work with officers from other nations.

During my tenure, I have worked with some exceptional police officers and civilian staff of all ranks and with others who were clearly deluded by their own capabilities. A quote from Plato comes to mind now; 'wise men speak because they have something to say; fools because they have to say something.'

Many of my colleagues paid the ultimate price for wearing the Harp and Crown, and many more sustained life-changing injuries, both physical and mental. There are those in our society, today, who are attempting to rewrite history, in line with their own agenda. What these officers and their families sacrificed for this province must never be forgotten.

When I was studying in London I played rugby at Rosslyn Park, so I am mindful of a quote from the late great Andy Ripley, former player with Rosslyn Park, England and the then British Lions, who lost his life to cancer. For me it is a universal quote that encompasses countless scenarios whether you are a believer or non-believer.

> Dare we hope? We dare. Can we hope? We can. Should we hope? We must, because to do otherwise is to waste the most precious of gifts, given so freely by God to all of us. So, when we do die, it will be with hope, and it will be easy, and our hearts will not be broken.

Now that you know a little bit about me, I want to take you inside the mind of a SOCO/CSI. I will share with you, from my own personal memories, some of the scenes that I forensically examined and reviewed.

This is not an exhaustive survey. It is more a series of snapshots, which will hopefully give you an insight into my experiences, both professional and personal, while always being mindful of others.

The events that you are about to read are not in any specific order. They are episodes, emerging from the stream of memory, asking to be heard.

# Chapter 2

# Annabella Symington

Mrs Symington was a quiet, wealthy, old age pensioner who lived alone after the death of her husband. She was a very private lady who took pride in her home in Willesden Park, a highly respectable suburb in south Belfast. This was a murder that hung over this leafy area of Belfast, like a dark cloud, for more than twenty years. There were no signs of forced entry and no disturbance inside her home.

She had opened the door, on Halloween night 1989, to someone that she knew or clearly trusted in the moment. The spectre that walked over the threshold of her door that evening choked her to death, forcing the sleeve of her cardigan down her throat. This crime was one of the most heinous unsolved crimes in Northern Ireland's history. It was a case that baffled detectives, who had done their utmost to solve it.

When I started at Ballyclare High School, Kenneth McConnell was in fifth year going into sixth year. If my memory serves me right, he was one of those senior pupils who had been presented with a maroon blazer.

These special blazers were worn by pupils who had, in the eyes of the teaching staff, excelled in a sporting endeavour or a field of study. This blazer was looked upon as a badge of honour within the school. The junior pupils were encouraged to try and achieve the same exacting standards as their seniors had achieved.

During my time at Ballyclare High School I played rugby, cricket, chess, poker, and pitch-and-toss. It was the pitch-and-toss that cost me the blazer when 'Big Jim,' the French teacher, caught us playing it one day.

We copped detention and we were also out of pocket because the coins went into the charity box. The moral of the story is that we should have employed a lookout during our break time endeavours. However, a lookout was not cheap in those days; a trip to the tuck shop was the fee.

When I moved to Ballyclare, in 1984, I enrolled my children in Ballyclare Primary School. The principal at that time was Mr Brown. Mr Brown's son and I were pupils, in the same year, at Ballyclare High School. We also played cricket in the first eleven, at both junior and senior level.

My son, during his time at primary school, made friends with a boy in his class who had the same Christian name, and they have stayed connected, from time to time, since their days at primary school. It was through my son's friend that I encountered Kenneth McConnell.

My wife and I got to know the parents of my son's friend and on occasions we would visit each other's homes. It was during one such visit that I was introduced to their next-door neighbour, Kenneth.

During my conversation with McConnell, he told me that he was a police officer. I was about to tell him that I too was in the police, but he beat me to the draw. It was clear that he had already been made aware of who I was.

I told him that I remembered him from my time at Ballyclare High School, but he did not recognise or remember me. I did not expect him to remember as we were several years apart. His persona was arrogant and overpowering. To me he looked as if he needed to always be in control. I knew there and then that he was someone to be ignored. This is the only time that we met and spoke to each other. In fact, I have never met or seen him in person again since that day.

However, during my police career, I was privy to several stories about him from other officers. If these stories were to be believed he was not on their Christmas card list. Little did I know it then, but the name Kenneth McConnell was to appear in front of me at a future date, and not in a good way.

In July 2007 I was the sole forensic reviewer in a new team, set up by the Police Service of Northern Ireland and based in Seapark, Carrickfergus. This team was given the name Retrospective Murder Review Unit (RMRU).

This new investigative and review team was comprised of serving PSNI officers of various ranks and retired police officers. The command structure was headed by three serving senior officers, three detective sergeants and three detective constables.

The retired officers were divided into four teams of four and my role was to undertake the forensic review of each case that a team was working on; that meant I could have four forensic reviews on the go at any one time.

If a case was a complex one the teams would merge. Few serving police officers, other than those involved, knew that there was a new investigative unit known as RMRU.

Having reviewed each case I would submit my findings, in writing, to the Senior Management Team. We also had an evidence search team consisting of retired police officers. The role of this team was to search for physical evidence at locations relevant to the case under review.

There was also an intelligence section, comprising two retired Special Branch officers, just in case we unearthed something that was beyond our pay grade.

Our remit was solely to review unsolved murders. It was the senior PSNI officers who made the decision as to which murder warranted a review. I had no input during this selection process. However, there must have been criteria in place for choosing one case over another.

With every position filled, we waited for the boss to blow the whistle so that the lid could be lifted off Pandora's Box. I knew that I would be dealing with complex cases that contained evil personified and much more.

I took time to consider how this new role would impact on my mental health, but as I had been recommended by the good old anonymous caller, I was obliged to pick up the gauntlet. I believed that if I could make a difference and help others it would be worth soaking in what the unknown had in store for me.

With my thoughts focused and my new pencils placed neatly in a row on my desk, I was like a coiled spring, ready for action; but there was a delay. The senior PSNI officer believed that a team building break, to the Lusty Beg Island Resort and Spa, was the way forward.

For those of you who have never heard of Lusty Beg Island it is an area of stunning natural beauty. It is a 75-acre private island in Lower Lough Erne, Co. Fermanagh, and the place is a refreshing escape from the turmoil of city life.

The trip was for all the serving police officers, with a former officer and I included. Prior to joining RMRU, this former officer had been a senior police officer in the PSNI training school at Garnerville, Belfast.

Shortly after arriving at Lusty Beg, we all met in the main building, where the SIO asked the former Garnerville trainer to employ his skills in making sure that the audio-visual equipment was functioning. When we had completed this task, the SIO looked at us and asked us to leave as he needed to discuss matters with his serving officers.

Around two hours later a runner was sent to invite us back, but we made an executive decision to remain seated. Also in our company, on this trip, were two American gentlemen, one from the Federal Bureau of Investigation and the other from the National Security Agency.

Those couple of days at Lusty Beg went well, but there was no team building exercise, at least none that I saw. Perhaps that was above my pay grade.

I was sitting at my desk in Seapark the following Monday morning when the rest of the team quizzed me about the team building trip. I replied with the standard formula;

'What happened in Lusty Beg stays in Lusty Beg.' Now back to the important matters.

During my two years in RMRU I reviewed numerous unsolved murder cases. All my written reports, some of which contained what I believed to be forensic opportunities, were submitted to the authorities, and in turn uploaded onto HOLMES 2 (Home Office Large Major Enquiry System). This is an information system used in the investigation of major incidents, such as the Annabella Symington case.

The system generates action sheets. Each action sheet is assigned to a specific investigator, detailing that person to carry out a task related to the investigation. When a task is completed the action sheet and the attached information are uploaded onto HOLMES2, which in turn generates another action, thus building a case, which the Senior Investigating Officer can review and drive forward.

The Seapark Complex in Carrickfergus was the ideal location for RMRU, as all the various forensic units and the police evidence storage facility were within its walls. During my police career I had met many forensic scientists, as we worked together hand in hand (and often on bended knees) at major crime scenes.

My new role gave me the opportunity to meet with familiar faces once again, though this time from behind a desk.

If I discovered what I believed to be a forensic opportunity to advance a particular case I could walk over to the lab, meet with one of my scientific friends and discuss the case. A face-to-face conversation was best, especially if there was a pastry and tea on offer.

It was near the end of 2008 when Geoff walked into the main office and over to my desk. Geoff was now a civilian, having been a senior ranked detective in a Scottish police force; he had joined RMRU some months after its inception.

Geoff asked me if I was available to discuss another case with him, so we retired to his office. At this point in time, I was working on two case reviews, so I was already busy. He handed me an envelope that had already been opened. I was about to remove its contents when he stopped me and asked me to listen to what he had to say before I read its contents.

Geoff informed me that the grandniece of a lady had written a letter to the Chief Constable, PSNI requesting a review of her aunt's murder. Her aunt was Annabella Symington.

He told me that this case had already been reviewed and there was nothing found that could further the investigation, but could I look at it anyway. I told him that the Symington murder was not on my list, but he asked me to make it a priority case, as this was a request from the Chief Constable. I was to organise a team to work on the Symington case; the other cases would have to take a back seat.

As I have already mentioned, there were four retired officers in each review team but in this case, there just happened to be a particular team that consistently produced investigative opportunities that fitted in with my forensic findings.

This team consisted of, in no particular order, Dick, George, Al, Tim (I do not do and). I called them (wait for it) the 'A Team.' Let us face it, you cannot be original every time. Sometimes the familiar works best. I told them that I had been given the Symington murder and that it was a priority case.

Like all my reviews the first port of call was the most recent review carried out by the Serious Crime Review Team.

At that time, such reviews contained everything there was to know about a criminal investigation, so they were a logical starting point. The role of this unit was to periodically review major criminal cases and, if new information became available, this would be acted upon accurately and promptly. The SCRT file concluded with what Geoff had already told me; there was nothing available to advance the investigation.

Armed with the background information I proceeded to carry out a review of all the forensic examinations and the evidence trail in the Symington case. I was hoping that there would be something, no matter how small, that I could get analysed for the presence of DNA from another source other than the deceased.

DNA was first used as an investigative tool in 1986 by DR. Alec Jeffreys, who had developed a DNA processing system in 1984. Genetic fingerprinting has been developed over the decades, and it has provided conclusive evidence in many court cases.

The Northern Ireland Forensic Science Laboratory (NIFSL), based in Newtownbreda, Belfast, at the time, was producing

Multilocus DNA Profiling and Single-Locus DNA profiling between 1988 and 1992.

In September 1992, a bomb detonated at NIFSL, causing extensive damage, so the laboratory moved to the Seapark complex, near Carrickfergus, and rebranded to become Forensic Science Northern Ireland (FSNI).

Another method used between 1992 and 2003 was DQa DNA Profiling. This analysis was more useful for crime scenes that only yielded tiny amounts of DNA material. The Northern Ireland DNA Database was established in 1996, with the National DNA Database having been established the previous year.

Current DNA analysis can produce a DNA profile from exceedingly tiny amounts of biological material, most of which are not visible to the human eye.

I had a system that I always adhered to when I was reviewing RMRU cases.
Once I had read the background information I would take a step back for an hour.

During this time, away from the case, I would go for a walk around the Seapark complex and call in at the FSNI canteen, where I would have a cup of tea and a conversation. Downtime over and brain rested, I would return to my desk and, with the documentation in hand, I would find an unoccupied room, where I would begin my forensic review. I would only leave that room to use the facilities, get a drink of water from the main office and lunch.

Free bottled water was the only job perk during my time in RMRU. (Oops! I forgot about the trip to Lusty Beg.) While I was getting water, Al or Tim would usually ask, 'Well, Ray, any nuggets yet?' I would reply 'not yet chaps,' or in the affirmative if I had struck gold. This became part of the office vocabulary, as I likened a forensic opportunity to finding a gold nugget.

Reviewing an historic unsolved murder case is complex in many ways and it should not be viewed in isolation. It is important that the review team also considers what resources were available to the investigators when the incident took place and if the workload, at the time, had a bearing on the investigation. It is so easy to be critical. Recommendations are best delivered through constructive criticism if I discover human error during a review.

Having reviewed the Symington case, I checked my notes again. I would always read my notes twice when reviewing a case, to make sure that I had considered everything. With draft review in hand, I returned to the office to be greeted with the usual nugget question. In this case I believed that I had struck gold; but more investigation was needed before I could be certain.

Even though I would check my work twice, in all cases under review, I would always hand the draft to the team for their comments.
This type of review work needs to be a team effort. I have seen too many times how someone believes that they have made a breakthrough and so they adopt the attitude that 'this is my idea and nobody else is getting a look-in.'

This type of tunnel vision has crashed and burned, on numerous occasions, because the hypothesis needed another piece to complete the jigsaw. Having read the forensic review my four amigos agreed with its content. However, was the potential evidence in the Symington case still available and if so, what condition was it in?

Even if exhibits from an historic case are available, it is not just a matter of handing them to a forensic scientist for examination. There are several matters to be considered before a scientific analysis takes place and if it takes place at all is dependent on the following: Contamination, Cross-contamination, Communication, and the Chain of Custody of all such evidence.

These four areas of crime scene investigation and forensic analysis are of vital importance if a prosecution is to stand a chance of being successful. Let me expand on these four terms.

**Contamination:** if the packaging that contains the potential evidence is broken open then the contents are contaminated.

**Cross-contamination:** if a CSI examines the main scene and then goes on to examine a second scene, which is believed to relate to the main scene, then there is every chance that trace evidence will be transferred to this second scene from the main scene. Wearing new personal protection equipment does not rule cross-contamination out.

**Communication:** it is vital that everyone involved in an investigation speak to each other as information comes into the enquiry. It may be the case that a specific piece of evidence needs to be prioritised for examination before everything else. In this case it was the fingernail scrapings of the deceased, as she may have scratched the culprit and her cardigan.

**Chain of custody:** this is a term used solely in connection with the recovery of potential evidence. For example, a CSI recovers an item at a scene and having sealed it in an evidence bag, he signs and dates the item. The next person who takes possession of this item signs and dates the item and this continues through to its conclusion. If this chain is broken then the item, which was important evidentially, becomes questionable as to its integrity. Chain of custody is to evidence as provenance is to a precious artwork.

The Four C's, as I call them, form a common thread that runs through all current and cold case investigations and reviews.

It is not merely a matter of reading the documentation in isolation; one must read it with the common thread in mind. If this thread is frayed, at any point, then the potential evidence in the case becomes investigative rather than prosecutorial.

In 1967, for those of you who are old enough to remember, the Grand National horse race at Aintree became famous throughout the world of horse racing and remains so to this day.

All the large fences had been jumped, and most of the field were still running. On the approach to what one would call a simple gorse fence disaster struck; numerous horses and jockeys fell. As a result of this error a horse called Fionavon, an outsider at 100/1, cleared the fence and went on to win the race. Here is my reason for using this analogy.

To prevent a Fionavon moment, where the defendant/s ride off into the distance because the case has fallen during trial, everyone involved — CSI, scientists, investigators, and the prosecution — must make sure that the common thread is not frayed before going to trial.

To mismanage a person's expectations is a recipe for disaster on all fronts. Unfortunately, human error occurs but a greater error is to try and bury a mistake, once it has been detected, or disguise it in some way.

Having reviewed the Annabella Symington case I was confident that the common thread was intact with regards to the original investigation. I contacted a member of staff at the evidence storage facility in Seapark, hoping that the fingernail clippings and cardigan, in the Symington case, were in cold storage; they were.

Armed with this information I submitted my report to the head of RMRU, recommending that the potential evidence in the Symington case be removed from the freezer in Seapark and delivered to a laboratory in England for DNA analysis. At this stage in my life, I had no idea how the Symington case was progressing as the PSNI dispensed with my services in 2009, shortly after my review.

In April 2010, I received a phone call from an RMRU colleague. This was the same former officer who first called me in 2007 and arranged for me to meet the head of RMRU.

Al's words were, 'Well done, you got McConnell for the Symington murder.' I was silent for a moment; then the emotion struck. What a result! I thanked him for calling me and thanked him again for his input into the Symington review. I told him that it had been a team effort.

Kenneth McConnell was arrested in October 1992 for the offence of extortion, for which he received a four-year jail sentence. As a result of this crime his DNA was uploaded to the NI DNA database.

In December 1992, another grandniece of the late Mrs Symington, and a friend of McConnell at this time, informed the police that she had suspicions that he may have been involved in her late aunt's murder. However, nothing came of this after police had investigated her complaint.

On 26th January 2010, the PSNI, armed with the new DNA results, which emanated from the cold case review, arrested Kenneth McConnell for the murder of Mrs Annabella Symington. Faced with this new DNA evidence, McConnell admitted to having killed this defenceless lady, in her home, on 31st October 1989 by choking her with the sleeve of her cardigan. He was the spectre that had entered her home.

So, there you have it. My connection to this case now extended beyond Ballyclare High School, Ballyclare Primary School, the parents of my son's friend and Kenneth McConnell.

Was the letter from her grandniece, who lived in Scotland, meant to come my way? Was divine intervention involved again? Life is full of occurrences and mysteries that we are yet to understand.

I have thought about this case over the years and about the last moments of Annabella's life, so when I read a newspaper article, in September 2018, I was again transported back to 2008, to when Geoff handed me the letter from her grandniece, who lived in Edinburgh.

In September 2018 there was an article printed in the Sunday World, a local newspaper. The Prison Service had temporarily released five convicted murderers, under supervision, so that they could 'enjoy a hike in the Mourne Mountains before going for a walk along Newcastle Promenade.'
One of these murderers was Kenneth McConnell.

I wonder if McConnell had a cup of tea during his sojourn in Newcastle and if so, did he reflect on the time that he sat at the tea table with Mrs Symington, prior to killing her and then stealing £200 from her. I would leave you to ponder if this thought crossed his mind. Personally, I very much doubt it.

This was a brutal murder of an elderly lady who had quite properly refused to provide McConnell with the means to continue funding his gambling addiction. McConnell had discovered that the South Belfast pensioner had money after he befriended her other grandniece, who was his next-door neighbour.

Mr Justice Hart sentenced McConnell as follows, 'I consider the appropriate period he should serve before he can be considered for release is eighteen years imprisonment. As is the normal practice this will include the time spent on remand.'

As you can see, there was no appendage stating that he could be released for a day at the seaside. Was the family of the late Mrs Symington ever informed that the person convicted of her murder was on a supervised day release to Newcastle? I doubt it.

Who decided that such a scheme is a clever idea? Giving convicted murderers a day out is one thing; but what adds fuel to the fire is that it was at the expense of the public purse. The next outing could be to the Giant's Causeway or better still, my personal favourite, the Carrick-a-Rede rope bridge, on a stormy day. In the words of Pink Floyd, I would 'lock the door and throw away the key.'

One of those in the 'Newcastle Five' was a William Mawhinney, who was convicted of the bathtub murder of a Lorraine Mills in Ballymena, another case that I reviewed while working in RMRU. In July 2009, the head of RMRU thanked me for my input but said that, due to budget issues, my services were no longer required, and a serving civilian CSI would be replacing me.

I never questioned this decision, but I was curious as to why the PSNI would remove a serving civilian CSI from an active crime scene unit, to take over from me at RMRU. To me this made no sense on financial or investigative grounds. Perhaps

I had brought matters into the light that were better left in the dark. I will never know.

Prior to leaving Seapark I met with the forensic scientists, with whom I had discussed several cold cases, and thanked them for their expertise and for taking time to listen to my findings. A team that has diverse investigative approaches at its disposal will be more creative and perform better.

When setting up a cold case review unit it is important that you employ people who bring different perspectives and cognitive diversity to an investigation because they may see opportunities that others have missed.

# Chapter 3

## The Shankill Bomb

Merely choosing the title for this chapter has filled my thoughts with the events that took place, at approximately one o'clock on that Saturday afternoon of 23rd October 1993. I was the Scenes of Crime Officer who examined this crime scene along with a forensic scientist from Forensic Science Northern Ireland.

There have been many articles written in newspapers, and television programmes produced, that one can read and view with regards to the carnage that took place at Frizzell's Fishmongers on the Shankill Road. I do not intend to repeat what has already been portrayed by the media. The 23 October 1993 started as an ordinary day, for many, on the Shankill Road, Belfast. However, the event that unfolded changed, unimaginably, the lives of many forever. A mass murder of local people.

I have a strong connection with the Shankill Road, on both a personal and professional level, and the associated scenes that I dealt with, weeks after that fateful day.

Let me turn the clock back to around 1960.

When I was a young child my mother drove a car, the colour of which is difficult to describe other than to place it in the beige spectrum. Anyway, the colour was not important to me at the time. I liked two things about this car. One thing fascinated me while the other brought me joy and, as my mother put it, kept me quiet for a while.

The car had two small, orange-coloured Bakelite signals that would pop out of the bodywork when employed. Sometimes my mother would turn them on for my amusement, but looking back it was done to keep me from repeating 'are we there yet?'

However, the main reason I liked this car was that it knew the way from the countryside to the sweet shop on the Shankill Road. With a little help from my mum, of course.

Once inside this sweet shop I would unleash the pennies and half-pennies from the pocket of my shorts, and stock up with Football Chums, a Bubbly, Rainbow Drops and the main feature, a sugar dummy, wrapped in cellophane and tied with a ribbon.

My sister got the ribbon, but I kept the plastic ring that held the ribbon to add to my collection. I was proud of my ring collection. I know what you are thinking, poor teeth.

No need to worry, my mum made sure I brushed my teeth three times daily. In the morning, after sweets, and at bedtime. I only wish that I had maintained this routine in the following years.

A Football Chum was a square, soft toffee wrapped in wax paper that had a football theme on the cover. The penny Bubbly was a round, pink chewing gum wrapped in multi-coloured wax paper. Rainbow Drops were multi-coloured puffed rice, and they were wrapped in a cone-shaped wax paper.

I had earned my pocket money by chopping sticks and weighing potatoes, which were sold in my parents' farm shop.

This trip would be repeated whenever I had saved enough pennies. The innocence of it all makes me wish that I could wrap myself in the safety net of what, for me and I am sure you, were better times.

There I was, on the Shankill Road, Belfast, with not a care in the world and munching through my sweets. My mother repeated this trip with my children, but in a car that had indicators and not trafficators; and pennies had been replaced by pounds. The sweet range changed but the sugar dummy was still available.

Tennent Street, for those who do not know it, is on the right as one drives up the Shankill Road from Belfast City centre. On entering Tennent Street, the police station is approximately six hundred meters ahead, on the left. The office where I worked is still being used, today, for the same purpose. In 1993 I was a SOCO, working out of Tennent Street RUC Station.

I will open the door to the SOCO office and invite you in for a short tour, but it is at your own risk. No Risk Assessment or Neutral Working Environment in those days. Officers in the upper echelons tried to introduce these two concepts into our office routine but, after careful consideration, for about two seconds, we did not see the need for change.

We start at seven on a typical day, and the office is full. The phones are ringing constantly, like slot machines emptying their coins onto the metal trays for the winners, but nothing major has been reported.

There are several heated debates taking place and some are complaining that they cannot hear what is being said on the phone. The language is colourful at times and not for the faint-hearted.

One needs to understand that this is a frontline unit, working in a daily cauldron of crime; sparks are bound to fly.

My detective colleagues once told me that our lively renditions could be heard a fair distance away and, depending on the level of noise, they would either call in, or have breakfast in the canteen first and call in on the way back for a discussion.

To the untrained eye the office environment was chaotic, but I can assure you there was no chaos involved, just strong-willed characters. The other office door opens, amid the noise, and a police officer informs us that there has been a shooting incident; you can hear a pin drop and everyone is instantly focused. As this officer is walking down the corridor, towards the front of the station, a SOCO team follows directly behind him.

I hope that this little insight has given you an idea of a typical day in my life as a SOCO, based at Tennent Street. Now, please close the door on your way out, I am off to do what I do best. I had been based in Tennent Street for just over three years, at this point in my career, with a heavy portfolio of trauma in tow, which matched the portfolios that some of my SOCO colleagues had to drag along. During this time, the Monday to Friday shift pattern was from seven to three and three to eleven; those finishing at eleven were on-call and available, on pager or the home phone, until seven the next morning.

I had eight statutory rest days per month, four-week days and two weekends.

That all sounds great, eight rest days built in; it never happened. In a typical month, on top of the normal hours, I usually had to work four of my eight rest days, four double shifts, two twelve-hour shifts and I was called out to attend scenes at least six times a month.

There were occasions when some of us slept in the office on weekends, due to continuous major incidents and volume crime scenes. Burglary, vehicle theft, and criminal damage are some examples of what is classified as volume crime scenes. I can see that some of you are wiping tears of sympathy from your eyes, while others are thinking 'well, he is being well paid.' Trust me I earned every penny, and I have the mental and physical scars as silent witnesses.

It was not out of choice that I had to work those extra hours, month in month out, it was a necessity for all of us, as the workload was heavy. There were times that I had so much overtime that I saved it in a 'toil bank.' I used this banked overtime to add on extra days to my annual leave and to top up my monthly salary when I was on leave.

My biggest regret was that I missed some family milestones, but this was not out of choice. 1993 was a year filled with milestones of a different nature. It was a year that I will never forget, but I was merely an observer and recorder of the hatred and atrocities that took place during that time.

It is now 22.45, Friday 22nd October 1993. I have just informed Belfast Regional Control, (BRC), that I will be on call from 23.00, on both pager and home phone. As I lock the office doors, at 23.00, and head to my car I am thinking what are the odds that my pager and home phone will remain silent for the next eight hours? This was the usual optimistic thought every time I was on call.

Here is what normally occurred; a pager message on the way home, or when I was at my front door, or a phone call while getting into bed, sometimes both pager message and phone when BRC wanted to make sure that I had been tasked.

On this occasion all remained silent, but that did not translate to a peaceful sleep. I described my sleep pattern, during on call periods, as 'what if' sleep; 'What if this happens?' Or 'What if that happens?'

I opened the office doors at seven o'clock, 23<sup>rd</sup> October 1993 and I hoped that the day that lay ahead would be uneventful; I was not called out to a scene.

By nine we had an extensive list of volume crime scenes to examine. I took my quota of jobs, contacted BRC to inform them which police division I would be working in, and headed off in one of the SOCO cars.

We had several cars in the unit, but none of them were head turners and none of them were armoured. We were expected to enter and leave police stations that only had armoured vehicles for their personnel. I was driving a Vauxhall estate car that was conspicuous by its colour, which I could only describe as phlegm green, but it was practical. The weather was mild and dry that day, as I examined stolen cars and burglary scenes.

Even though such scenes were not classed as being major, in SOCO terms, they were none the less major in the eyes of those who had their car stolen or home invaded. I always treated volume crime scenes with the same amount of professionalism, dedication, and empathy as the major crime scenes that I had examined.

Lunch time was beckoning and to my astonishment I had not been tasked to a major incident, so I bought food and headed back to the office. It was the norm, due the workload, to 'eat on the hoof.'

I stopped the SOCO car, on the Shankill Road, waiting for a break in the traffic, so that I could turn right onto Tennent Street. The traffic heading past me towards Belfast city centre was constant; then it happened. I heard a loud noise behind me, and when I looked in the rear-view mirror I could see that the air was heavy with smoke, some 150 meters away. My initial thought was that this explosion was the result of a gas leak. However, my SOCO instincts were telling me something else. The Shankill Road, on a Saturday, is usually packed with shoppers and this was the case on 23$^{rd}$ October 1993. In less than a minute there was a large crowd working frantically to extricate those who were under the mound of rubble that had once been Frizzell's Fishmongers.

The screams of those who were injured filled the air; children were crying, and large crowds of bystanders were gathering. It was not long before chaos became organised chaos as the crowd, including uniformed police officers, continued to search the rubble for bodies.

It was like a well-oiled machine; everyone recovered the bodies from the rubble.
Firefighters arrived followed by ambulances and a person driving a JCB digger. The JCB was worth its weight in gold, as it removed heavy rubble to allow better access.

Paramedics were helping the injured before taking them to hospital; they were also removing bodies from the scene. Preservation of life always comes first in such circumstances, even if potential evidence is trampled.

While this was taking place, I was quietly searching underneath and around vehicles, which were parked close to the scene, in case a secondary device had been planted. Having cleared the surrounding area, I ushered a crowd of people further back from the perimeter of the blast. I asked these people to speak to other members of the public as they walked towards the scene.

The benefit of this task was twofold; it kept the crowd back from the bomb site and diverted their thoughts, for a while, away from the horror further down the road. It was not long before all the injured and those who had not survived the blast were removed. More police officers were arriving, and the scene was being managed at this point.

The cordons were now in place and there was nobody within the tapes. At this point I returned to where I had abandoned the SOCO car to suit up for a closer look at the scene; I noticed that I had left the key in the ignition. Suitably dressed in my protective overalls and hard hat, I checked in with the log officer and officially entered the scene.

An eerie silence had descended over the area as I stood on the Shankill Road, facing the shattered remains of the shop.

Brick dust, from the blast, had soaked in the blood like sawdust does on a butcher's floor.

I closed my eyes in prayer for a moment then engaged my SOCO brain and set about preparing the scene for examination. I consulted with the police officer in charge to make sure that the duty forensic scientist had been tasked, along with a photographer and mapper. I then arranged to have extra police officers equipped with shovels and brushes to attend at the cordon.

I was not aware, at this stage, that the two people responsible for this savagery were part of the crime scene, one having been killed and the other injured.

The police photographer and mapper arrived, followed by the forensic scientist. When all three were suitably attired and logged into the scene I briefed them on what had taken place, thus far. Time was marching on, and the light was starting to fade. When the photographer and mapper had finished, I handed crime scene suits to a group of police officers, who had shovels and brushes, and supervised them as they organised the debris, outside the inner cordon, into manageable piles.

When darkness finally descended, over this awful scene, we all logged out, removed our PPE (Personal Protection Equipment), and returned to Tennent Street, RUC Station for a debrief.

I had arrived on the Shankill Road around one o'clock and left just before nine. I spent the next hour in Tennent Street RUC station, where a plan of action was discussed for the next day. I washed my face and hands and cleared my nose and throat, but the smell from the scene was ingrained in my senses and clothing. I smelt of fish and brick dust.

The drive home was filled with thoughts of what had taken place and what I needed to do the next day at the crime scene. I arrived home late, having remembered extraordinarily little about the journey home, to be greeted by my wife; after I had uttered the words 'What a day,' she knew that I had been at the Shankill Road bomb scene. Shower time.

I did not expect to have any sleep that night, but it was quite the opposite. My wife told me that I was sound asleep in a matter of minutes.

When I was getting ready to leave the next morning, she told me that I sat upright in bed, around two o'clock, shouted at the top of my voice for about ten seconds, without waking up, and then lay back down again. She told me that my utterance contained no words of English. How strange.

All agencies met in Tennent Street RUC Station that Sunday, 24th October, before returning to the crime scene. Lorries, an excavator, and a crane had been organised to remove large pieces of debris that we had examined at the scene. The smaller debris was loaded into skips for later examination by a specialist forensic team.

Several hours into the examination everything, up to the entrance of the shop, had been cleared. At this point we decided to have a short break; that was when we were briefed that there were two bombers; one was killed inside the premises while the other was injured.

Once break was over, I commenced a fingertip search of what remained of Frizzell's. During this fingertip search I picked up a clump of matted hair, which held my gaze for a time before I snapped back to reality.

Fingertip search over and potential evidence bagged, we walked out of the premises and onto the Shankill Road. I stood in silence for a moment, looking back into the void and the surrounding area where nine innocent people had been murdered and many more injured. I then walked over to the scene log officer but before I signed out, I turned to take a last look at where two members of the Provisional IRA, had carried out this needless act of violence.

After a short debrief, in the SOCO office, we all went our separate ways. What would Monday bring? It was normal practice to restock a SOCO car with new equipment after a major scene examination, but I figured that could wait until the morning. On this occasion I locked both car keys in my desk drawer; I had a personal reason for keeping the car locked.

Anyway, there were three other SOCO cars available. I arrived in the office around nine having had a weekend best forgotten, as if my mind would let that happen. I told Jim, the senior SOCO, to take me off scene duty as I had work to complete from the weekend. I also had a more important task to complete, which I kept private.

There was no rank structure in SOCO, at the time, but Jim ran the office exceptionally well and we answered to the Detective Inspector, CID, Tennent Street.

There was plenty of dark humour and funny moments, during my years in Tennent Street. Dark humour and alcoholic beverage acted as foils against adversity yet again. In the absence of such an outlook, and I am in no doubt of this, specialist units within the NHS would have been more than gainfully employed by our attendance.

Now back to the tasks in hand.
Having completed the paperwork with respect to the Shankill bomb, I had one more task to finish. I needed a small lockable drawer, and I knew where to get one. The local intelligence officer had small metal drawer units in his office, which were used to house index cards.

This officer did not have a spare drawer but when I told him why I needed it he removed the index cards and handed one to me, along with a key to lock it. Having placed the drawer on my desk I went out to the SOCO car, removed a paper evidence bag from the boot and returned to my desk.

The paper evidence bag contained a single brick from the Shankill bomb scene, which I gently removed and placed in the metal drawer, on top of tissue. I was the only person in the office at the time. I locked the drawer and placed the key on top.

However, I should have known better.

Not thinking, I had made what would turn out to be a schoolboy error by leaving the key on the top of the box. This brick was impressed with, Heatheryknowe Patent Glasgow. So, why did I take it? I recovered it as a mark of respect and a way of self-coping.

Around lunch time the following day, I was in the office talking about the Shankill Road scene to colleagues when one of them asked to see what was in the box. I opened the box to find that someone had used a red permanent marker to autograph the brick with the name 'Billy.' Some of the red colour remains on the surface.

This produced the desired result. Fuse having been lit I went off on a rant that was not Sunday school material. When I landed back on earth I took note of the writing style, removed what I could from the brick, locked it in the box and took the box home at the end of duty. The brick is currently in 'Decorum NI,' a Northern Ireland based charity, as part of a permanent display.

It took me a while to compare the writing on the brick with that of my colleagues, but I succeeded in getting a match. What happened next is a story for another day. Payback was achieved.

I recently met with a former police officer who was one of the first responders to the scene on the Shankill Road. It is important to provide you with his account of events and the role that he played at this scene, and I have his permission to do so. Here is his account.

> My colleagues and I were sitting in a police Land-rover, which was parked in Royal Avenue, Belfast, when I heard a loud explosion. I was about to search the channels, on the police radio, when Belfast Regional Control came on the air requesting if anyone was free to attend the scene of an explosion on the Shankill Road.

Royal Avenue, Belfast is a short distance from the Shankill Road so, with blue lights flashing and siren wailing, we responded to the request. We were on the lower Shankill in under a minute and heading to the scene. I could see vehicles reversing down the Shankill, towards us, as we approached at high speed.

Having dodged these cars, which had impeded our approach, I alighted from the Land-rover as the driver applied the brakes and brought the vehicle to a shuddering halt. About two minutes had passed between receiving the request and my boot contacting the road surface at the scene.

A colleague instinctively grabbed our first aid box, but it was clearly redundant. The scene in front of me was chaotic. I had only taken a few steps, onto a mound of rubble, when a male person, known to me, grabbed hold of my police jumper and punched me in the face. He accused me of letting this happen.

I thought 'what an idiot.' There was no time for this nonsense, so I pushed him out of the way and started to remove rubble, by hand, in the hope of finding survivors.

People were screaming in pain and despair. This primal scream, which came from deep within, intensified as they watched the events unfold in front of them.

The scene was now one of organised chaos. I quite quickly realised that there were several fatalities. I looked up, at this point, and noticed a senior officer, in full uniform, across the road. I shouted to him to ask if he could organise body bags to be conveyed to the scene.

He told me that the firefighters could provide the body bags. I ignored his response and continued searching. That was two idiots that I had dealt with that day. All the agencies had arrived by now and everyone was working in unison as the search continued.

As I was helping to remove a body from the rubble, I realised that I knew this gentleman. I had taken a statement from him, some years ago, in reference to a minor traffic accident. It was the body of Mr Frizzell. Bodies were placed onto ambulance trollies and removed from the scene. I then noticed a JCB arriving at the scene and the driver used his machine to remove heavy rubble to allow us better access.

While searching through the last area of rubble I found the remains of another body. I found out later that this was the body of the bomber, Thomas Begley.

The search of the rubble ended; adrenaline was still coursing through my body. I looked down at my bare hands and uniform. My hands, like many other hands, were cut and raw but the pain had stayed silent until the search had ended. Preservation of life was paramount; injured hands were a small price to pay.

My police uniform was covered in human remains, fish and brick dust, but it could be replaced. Nine innocent people were murdered on that day, and they can never be replaced.

The following week I arrived at the clothing store in Seapark, Carrickfergus, to obtain a new uniform, with my stained uniform suitably sealed in a bag. The person receiving my old uniform believed it only needed a wash, and it would be OK. The fact that I had worn it at the Shankill Road bomb scene appeared not to have registered.

Without going into the finer detail, I eventually got a new uniform. This scene has caused me sleepless nights over the years and has been brought back to the surface many times since.

However, and despite the passage of time I found it therapeutic; having been given an opportunity to unburden my thoughts to my former SOCO colleague.

A few days had passed since the Shankill Road bomb incident when I received a request to attend Antrim Road RUC station, Belfast and speak to CID.

A shooting had occurred in Ardoyne, Belfast. An army private had fired his weapon at a group of mourners standing outside the home of the late Thomas Begley, former member of the

Provisional IRA, who had carried the bomb into Frizzell's Fishmongers.

The Investigating Officer left instructions that I was to carry out a forensic examination on this army private for the presence of cartridge discharge residues to confirm that he had used a firearm.

I introduced myself to the man and explained to him what was involved in my examination. When I had finished, I handed my exhibits to a CID officer based in Antrim Road RUC Station. This trooper had discharged his firearm, before his colleagues disarmed him. He had used the pipe range for firearms training but not in the days before the funeral.

Why did I need to swab him? Well, I suppose an order is an order, after all. Several thoughts came into my mind during this up close and personal examination, but I invoke the basic human right of privacy, so 'no comment.'

In November 1993, a Detective Sergeant contacted me and asked me to meet him for a briefing regarding Sean Kelly, the Provisional IRA bomber, who was injured while helping Begley. Kelly was in a private room in the secure wing of

Musgrave Park Hospital, Belfast and the SIO required me to obtain a sample of his buccal cells (these are contained inside the mouth) and head hair for forensic analysis.

Several weeks had passed since my examination on the Shankill Road, so there was no concern with regards to cross contamination. A member of staff opened the door to the private room, and I entered, accompanied by a Detective Inspector and Detective Sergeant from CID Tennent Street. The D/Sgt spoke to Kelly and then it was over to me.

I had a personal approach when dealing with this type of examination. I would place the entire routine in the OCD spectrum. At this point, the detectives excused themselves and left the room. Kelly was sitting upright on the bed with one feature that my eyes were instantly drawn to. He had a crusty section of skin, which had once been part of his top lip, resting on his bottom lip, but still just attached to his top lip at one end. Buccal swab barrier? I do not think so!

This was going to be another time where I would need to remain calm and professional. Step closer and observe as the examination begins.

I fixed my gaze on Kelly and commenced as follows:

'Mr Kelly, I am a police officer and what I require from you is a sample of buccal cells from the inside of your mouth, and a sample of your head hair, in connection with the explosion at Frizell's Fishmongers, Shankill Road, Belfast, on 23$^{rd}$ October 1993. Will you consent in writing under the Police and Criminal Evidence Act to provide these samples?'

Kelly remained silent. I signed, dated, and entered the time of refusal on the PACE form. I continued, 'Mr Kelly I have the right, under PACE, to obtain these samples by force if necessary.' Kelly again remained silent as he stared back at me.

I noticed that he had something in his mouth, which I asked him to remove; he refused. I noticed Everton Mints on the locker, to his right, so I assumed it was a mint. Then I advised him, 'Mr Kelly if you do not remove the sweet from your mouth I will remove it.'

On hearing this Kelly removed the sweet. It was indeed an Everton Mint. I then commenced with my examination of Kelly and obtained the necessary samples. Lying on a bed in front of me was someone who was responsible for the murder of nine people and the injury of over fifty more and to me there was no visible sign of regret. His silent anger and hatred showed in his eyes throughout the examination.

Before leaving the room, I thanked Mr Kelly for his cooperation and told him that he was free to finish his Everton Mint.

The samples were delivered to the forensic science laboratory for examination. This was yet another psychological string tying me to the events on the Shankill Road, as if I needed a reminder.
Fast forward several weeks.
One day I noticed a large group of people in the Tennent Street canteen. It was so packed that it was standing room only. I asked one of the uniformed officers what was happening, and he told me that the Superintendent had invited those personnel who had helped during the Shankill bomb, and some of the local community, for an afternoon tea. This was a thoughtful decision to make.

There was no invite for my two SOCO colleagues who attended the postmortem examinations on the nine innocent people who were murdered by Begley and Kelly, and no invite for me. Not that we needed an invite, but the recognition of our work would have been appreciated.

However, the boss and I passed each other outside the SOCO office the next day and I thanked him for his invite. I like to think that the penny dropped as I walked on to attend another crime scene.

Whoever was in the shadows knew that such an attack on the protestant community would perpetuate violence and that is exactly what happened.

During my retirement I contacted a former colleague, who is at present still working as a CSI. The reason for this call was that we had worked as part of a team during an investigation into a murder that took place in East Belfast.

I had examined the main scene, while he examined an associated scene in the same building. He agreed to meet me, and he gave me his permission to include details of what he could recall in connection with this murder (see chapter 6).

During our conversation I spoke about the Shankill Road bomb scene, and he informed me that he was at the scene shortly after the explosion. When he agreed to meet me, he told me that he could only stay for an hour. A phone call was made and this hour turned into four hours and six cups of coffee.

I bought the coffee. I asked him to recall his actions at the scene of this mass murder. The following is his account.

During the morning of Saturday, 23rd October 1993 I had been at Perrie Park, Belfast, covering a school rugby match, as I was a voluntary first aid provider with St John's Ambulance.

The match ended without incident, so it was time to return to the depot in Mayo Street, Belfast, which is near the top of the Shankill Road.

I was about to turn left into Mayo Street when I heard an explosion, behind me, followed by a dust cloud coming towards me. I turned the ambulance around and headed down the Shankill Road towards the scene.

When I parked, I could see a large crowd moving rubble, and walking wounded, who were staggering and clearly dazed. I had dealt with other incidents that involved the loss of life but nothing on this scale.

My colleague and I attended to the wounded, in order of priority, while waiting for ambulances to arrive. Most of the wounded went to the Mater Hospital in private cars and ambulances; but due to the number of people injured others went to the Royal Victoria Hospital.

I returned to the rubble to help, and it was not long before everything had been done that could be done, with respect to the recovery of those innocent people who were killed because of this explosion.

Having done what I could, I stood facing the scene and reflected on what had occurred. Covered from head to toe in brick dust, my colleague and I walked back to where I had parked the ambulance.

Seven years after this atrocity I was successful in my application to join a crime scene investigation unit in

Belfast, where I worked alongside the author of this narrative, at several major crime scenes.

Recalling this incident, in the presence of someone who understands the fallout from such a scene, was good for my mental wellbeing. Now back to fighting crime.

The years have passed swiftly, during my retirement, and since that day on the Shankill Road, but my thoughts of what took place have not diminished, nor has my loathing for those who organised and carried out that vile murder of innocents. The misplaced logic and theories behind why this atrocity was perpetrated can be read in several published articles, available on the internet.

The following story informs the reader about the life of a gentleman, and my friend, who was born in Malvern Street, an area off the Shankill Road, Belfast, known as "The Hammer." For locals, it was viewed as a bastion of invincibility. There are several theories why this area got its name but none of them conclusive.

I was one of nine children living in a two-bedroom house, so you can imagine the conditions that we faced. Times were hard. The area was coming down with children playing street games, not aware of the hardships that our parents faced, daily. I am sure that many of you will remember; knock the door, stick in the mud, hide, and seek and many more. We made our own fun. The innocence of youth.

There were many atrocities during my formative years and lives were lost on both sides. I witnessed the aftermath of explosions that took numerous lives, for example, 'Wee Joe's' cinema and the 'Bayardo Bar,' to name but two. As a result of these terrorist attacks the ranks of the local paramilitary organisations increased without the need for a recruiting Sergeant. I made the conscious decision not to venture down that road.

There is a proud history of military service in my family.

My great grandfather was in The Royal Inniskilling Fusiliers and then joined the 24th Regiment of Foot at Rorke's Drift, where the regiment defended the mission station during the Anglo-Zulu War. He received a military funeral up the Shankill Road, Belfast, with the coffin, containing his remains, resting on a gun carriage. What an honour!

My grandfather and his three brothers fought in WW1, having joined The Royal Irish Rifles.

My father was in the Royal Navy along with his brother.

I joined the Ulster Defence Regiment which merged with The Royal Irish Rangers, to form The Royal Irish Regiment.

My son of whom I am extremely proud not only for being my son, but also for becoming a Royal Marine Commando. He served in Northern Ireland and the second Gulf War.

I joined the armed forces to help bring about an end to the terrorist war that was taking place in my back yard. This war for whatever reason went under the heading of 'The Troubles.' Shame on those who never looked upon such carnage as a War.

If you ask anyone who served in the British Army, the RUC and the UDR/RIR they will tell you that they fought in a war against terrorists. The Provisional IRA and other terrorist organisations will also tell you that they fought a war against the security forces, whom they saw as the enemy and still do.

We were on a war footing. 'The Troubles' what bright spark produced that degrading description. We won this war against terrorism and those terrorists who survived can thank 'The Good Friday Agreement' for coming to their rescue.

These are my views on what took place in my back yard.

The first casualty of war is the truth.

I would like to finish my story on a lighter note. A blast from the past.

It was around 2200, and my colleagues and I were lying in a field outside a town called Bessbrook, having relieved an army unit based in that area. We informed the local police that we were in position waiting for their arrival to set up a vehicle check point.

It was a cold clear night when we settled into position. Radio silence was broken by the point man who uttered the word, "contact."

He spotted what he believed was someone moving in a nearby field. The commanding officer on looking through his night sight confirmed that it was a scarecrow. The radio operator replied, "should I call for backup sir" to which the officer replied, "it is only a fucking scarecrow why would we need backup" Well sir there could be two of them." Dark humour at its best.

# Chapter 4

## No Longer Here

In this chapter I will give you an insight into some of the suicide, sudden death, and accidental death scenes that I have attended. I will also include the most heinous of all crimes, murder.

In such circumstances the coroner needs to know who the deceased was, when the deceased died, where the deceased died and how the deceased died. In all cases, where a postmortem is required, it is the pathologist who will officially confirm the cause of death, if one can be established.

It may be one factor or many factors that makes someone decide that life is not worth living. I have only seen and dealt with the aftermath of such a decision and the various means employed when someone intentionally takes their own life.

Did I ever get used to dealing with such scenes? Well, the simple answer is never, especially if a child or young person had died.

I have placed my hand on the head of an infant and closed my eyes and I have held the hand of a deceased gentleman, in his eighties and closed my eyes, and there have been many in between this age range. The assumption that tomorrow will be OK is a fragile tissue of hope.

The role of a Scenes of Crime Officer in suicide, sudden death and accidental death is to examine these scenes to rule out any visible signs of foul play and to assist the local police officer in his or her investigation.

When I attended such scenes, I would always make sure that my advice and actions did not undermine the capabilities of the investigating officer (IO). One needs to have exceptional social skills in these circumstances as a word out of place can cause even more distress.

I hear you asking, what does he mean? Surely such an occurrence is a tragedy beyond comprehension. You are right but, trust me, a raised voice, or careless words, in a home where a loved one has died, is something that will never be forgotten. One does not learn these life skills overnight, or at a two-week course in a police training college.

On arrival at a scene of alleged suicide I would always ask the IO to join me, away from everyone, so that we could discuss the investigation in private: what has been done, what remains to be done, what needs to be removed as evidence and what experience does the IO have in dealing with such a scene. We all had to learn.

I have attended many suicides, sudden deaths, and some accidental deaths during my career. Sometimes a postmortem can change the direction of an investigation; what was considered not to be a suspicious death at the time, becomes suspicious due to the postmortem results.

During my career I was given the opportunity to attend a Disaster Victim Identification workshop (DVI), in England. There were eight of us in a room discussing and reviewing two major cases: the Zeebrugge ferry disaster of 1987 and the 2004 south-east Asia Tsunami. One person in the group was a SOCO at the Zeebrugge scene and another was part of an international team of scene investigators that dealt with the aftermath of the Tsunami. This workshop provided me with an insight into tragedy on a massive scale and the extreme difficulties encountered by those who examined these scenes.

I was three months into my two-year probation period, as a uniform police officer, when my section Sergeant asked me to drive him to the scene of a sudden death. On the way to the house, he told me that I would be in charge, and he would guide me through the investigation.

As we were walking towards the front door of the property, around three in the afternoon, a gentleman approached and told us that he had phoned the police, because he had not seen his elderly neighbour leave her home that morning and she had a set routine each day.

We checked the doors and windows for any sign of a forced entry and all appeared normal. There was a top opening upstairs window ajar, at the front of the house, but ladders would be needed to access it. As luck would have it, this gentleman had ladders. Having obtained the ladders, the question was who was going to climb them?

For me, the Sergeant was the obvious choice. I was younger but he had longer arms, which he put to good use by reaching in to access the latch on the side window.

We were both standing in the front hallway some two minutes later. I returned the ladders and thanked the gentleman. The Sergeant informed me that the lady was deceased in her bedroom.

While the Sergeant was arranging for a Force Medical Officer to pronounce life extinct, I walked up the stairs towards the bedroom. This was my first sudden death scene. I stood at the entrance to the main bedroom, from where I could see the body of an elderly lady, in her dressing gown, face down and draped over the bottom of the bed.

I went back downstairs and after searching the drawer of a small table in the hallway I found a phone number, which I rang. The lady who answered the phone arrived a brief time later, introduced herself and she talked about her aunt's life, as I listened intently. What a fascinating life she had lived. Her late husband had been in the Royal Irish Constabulary and there was a photograph of him, in his uniform, standing beside his horse. I thanked her for sharing such details. The postmortem results showed that the lady had died of natural causes.

A few weeks later I was in the delivery room in the Jubilee Maternity Hospital, Belfast, waiting for the birth of my daughter. I am in no doubt that some of you will remember Jubilee, which no longer exists; but there is a beautiful statue located where the entrance steps to the building used to be.

As I stood in the delivery room, the door opened and a lady wearing an all-white uniform looked into the room then left. Much to my amazement, it was the niece who had told me about her late aunt's life.

Around ten minutes later she entered the room again, handed me a cup of tea and biscuits, then left. A nurse, who was standing beside me, remarked, 'That's a first; no one has ever been given tea and biscuits.' The other nurse asked me if I knew matron; I told them that I had never met her before.

Confidentiality is extremely important, so telling a harmless lie, in this case, was acceptable. The kind gesture was her way of saying thank you.

This lady and my mother had two things in common; they had the same Christian names, and they were midwives. What a coincidence, or was it another one of life's meant to be moments? Who knows! I believe that such occurrences happen for a reason.

There was only one sudden death scene where my advice was disregarded. It was the death of an infant in a cot. I offered advice but the officer in charge insisted that he had everything under control. I was even cut off in mid-sentence, so I left the scene in his capable hands.
I found out later that when the coroner asked the officer if he had drawn a sketch of the infant in the cot the officer's reply was no.

The coroner reported the matter to his superiors. I did my best. This officer attained the rank of Sergeant. I thought he might have gone further up the chain of command.
The postmortem results concluded that this was a case of sudden infant death syndrome (SIDS).
Walking into a room to find that your pride and joy has passed away must be one of the most traumatic events in any parent's life. It is soul altering.

This next case involves the death of a young person and like all deaths involving children and young people it is not only a tragedy in the present, but also the loss of the future.

The word why only contains three consonants but the metaphorical weight it carries makes it one of the heaviest, psychologically, and physically damaging words in our vocabulary.
Suicide is an extremely complex issue and when a person makes the intentional decision to take their own life it devastates families and friends. Those who are left behind, in the aftermath of suicide, go through an agony of self-interrogation, searching for a reason: why did this happen?

I was paged to a property in Belfast where a teenager had ended his life by hanging, using an electrical extension lead. The teenager's body had already been removed prior to my arrival.
As I approached the front door of the property it opened and a police officer invited me into the hallway, where he started to brief me on what had taken place. While standing in the hallway I could hear adults talking in a downstairs front room, to my right, so I spoke softly and told him that it would

be best to go outside to discuss matters. This request was ignored.

It was instantly clear to me that he saw himself as being in charge and he needed to explain things there and then.

When he was explaining that the suicide took place in an upstairs bedroom, I seized my opportunity and quietly ushered him upstairs. I had managed to remove his physical presence from the eyes and ears of the people in the front room.

As he started to explain things in more detail, I told him to lower his voice as 'walls have ears.' It was a lost cause. Then he gave me his version of events. The teenager tied an electrical extension lead to a coat hanger rail, on the inside of his bedroom door, put his head into the loop and took his own life.

I looked at the coat hanger rail, the extension lead and the bedroom and told him that he was almost right. He was not a happy chap.

I explained that the scene examination needed to be accurate to provide information for the pathologist, the coroner and most importantly the family. I agreed that the young man had indeed used the extension lead to end his life, but I suspected that his first attempt had failed, when the top of one of the coat hooks snapped.

He went to the next hook and this time, sadly succeeded in taking his own life. The police officer disagreed but when I pointed out a small metal fragment on the bedroom floor below the rail and the broken hook between the bed and bedside locker, the penny dropped.

I have often thought; what if the other coat hook had broken? Would this have stopped him in his tracks? That is something that we will never know.

I was not looking for a thank you; a mere 'I think you are right' would have sufficed.
The management of this scene showed a lack of social skills coupled with arrogance. However, I got there in the end.

Before leaving the family home I knelt beside his mother and, holding her hand and arm, I told her that I was deeply sorry for her loss. I would always pass on my condolences at such a scene if an opportunity arose. The results of the postmortem concluded that this young man had taken his own life.

I have attended many scenes of suicide where firearms have been the choice to end life. I do not feel that it is necessary to paint you a picture of such a scene as I am sure that you have seen suitably graphic imitations while watching television dramas.
There was one such scene during my career as a SOCO, where the person who wanted to end his life thankfully survived.

A young police officer and his fiancé had split up, so he decided to end his life. Having chosen a suitable location, he put the barrel of his personal issue firearm in his mouth and pulled the trigger. The weapon discharged but the bullet, thankfully, exited below his left eye socket.
I met this officer some years later and dark humour filled the air. I remarked that the scar did nothing for his looks and he responded with 'well at least I am alive.' We had a chin wag,

which contained some more dark humour, and then went our separate ways.

It was a bright sunny Saturday afternoon, and I was driving to the next job on my list when my pager broke the silence. Police needed me to attend the scene of a shooting, and could I meet the detective in charge of the incident at his office?

I walked into the CID office a short time after receiving the request. The detective in charge of this case made me tea and, while I was drinking it, he started to brief me on what had happened. I set aside my tea in a matter of seconds. The tone of his voice, his body language, and the empathy that he displayed, throughout this briefing, was something to behold.

I am not going to take you through this scene step by step. A brief outline will provide you with all the information of how an avoidable event unfolded in this family home.
Are you sitting comfortably?

A young man had always wanted to become a soldier and when he was old enough, he applied. His application was successful and, having passed basic training, which included weapon training, he was qualified to carry a personal issue handgun.

The weekend beckoned and he had the Saturday off, so he called to see his parents, to let them know that he was enjoying army life. It was during this visit home that tragedy struck. His father wanted to hold his son's handgun, so he passed it over, having made it safe to handle; or so he thought. Unfortunately, the weapon had not been made safe.

His father pointed the weapon in the direction of his wife, who was only a few feet away, and pulled the trigger, believing that the weapon was safe. There was a round in the breech, which discharged; the bullet struck his wife in the head, resulting in her instant death.

It was not my place to apportion blame; my role in this case was to carry out a forensic examination of the scene. When I arrived at the property, I was met by another detective, who briefed me again. The only people remaining at the scene were police officers. Having signed into the scene log and suitably attired in my forensic outfit, I entered the house. Life had been pronounced extinct by a police doctor and her body had been removed prior to my arrival.

The layout of this semi-detached property, which butted the footpath, was compact. The small room where the tragedy unfolded was the first room to my right, as I walked down the narrow hallway.

Before beginning my examination, I stood in this room, looking out the window at the traffic passing by, thinking that there was life passing by, oblivious as to what had taken place in this family home. I doubted that it would ever be a family home again.

I have numerous tragic events stored away in my shiny galvanised bin, but now and then something escapes, and I must corral it once more before things get out of control.

In this case it was the cream-coloured crepe bandage that had been wrapped around the wound on this lady's head. The seepage of blood had stained this bandage a shade of pink, in places, as her body lay stretched out in the mortuary waiting for the pathologist to arrive. I can visualise it now.

This next scene is one that will leave you thinking about life and the cruel way it can suddenly drop you into an abyss of darkness.

It was Christmas Eve 1997, and the presents were under the tree. I was looking forward to going home and leaving food out for Santa and the reindeers and doing things that fathers do at this time of the year, like taking a bite out of the mince pie and drinking some of Santa's milk.

All was peaceful but then the office phone rang. Before answering the call, I thought, please let this be someone looking for advice over the phone.

It was Belfast Regional Control to inform me that police required my presence at a local hospital; the case concerned the accidental death of a young teenager, and they told me I would be briefed on arrival.

I had examined numerous scenes where life had been extinguished. Nonetheless, this scene rocked me to my core and still does. When I pushed open the entrance doors to a general ward, on the first floor, I noticed crime scene tape and a police officer holding a bright yellow coloured scene log. I introduced myself and signed into the log.

I could tell by his voice that this officer was stressed. We moved to a quiet corner, just inside the tape, were I asked him to brief me on what had occurred. His voice faltered near the end of the briefing, and I reassured him that he had done an excellent job.

A patient on the ward was supposed to get home for Christmas, so his wife and son arrived to collect him. However, prior to their arrival he started to feel unwell, so the medical staff decided that he needed to remain in hospital until his health improved.
This must have been a disappointment but everyone no doubt understood.
After some time waiting, their son started to feel light-headed, so his mum told him to go into the ward's communal area. This area was like an annex, at the side of the ward, where the air was cooler, and people could have a quiet moment with their thoughts.

This open annex had a metal-framed, veranda-style room attached to it. The veranda could be accessed via a metal framed and glazed door. The top half of this annex and veranda was glazed with safety glass and the bottom half was glazed with glass that was reinforced with fine steel mesh, what they call Georgian style wired glass.

As you know, hospital wards are always busy with medical staff doing what they do best, and at visiting times the noise on the ward is increased. However, a loud noise coming from outside the ward alerted staff; they hurried into the communal area, where they were faced with a life-taking medical emergency.

The teenager had collapsed from a standing height and his head had struck a panel of reinforced glass with a force so great that it was heard above all other noises in the area. Medical staff did all that they could, at the point of impact and on the operating table, but the young man sadly passed away.

I was writing my scene notes when the uniform officer in charge of the case arrived. He apologised for not being available. I told this officer that an apology was not necessary but what was necessary was for him to sit down and gather his thoughts.
I approached him once he had rested, and we discussed the scene.

He had most things covered and agencies tasked. I told him to note down the constantly flickering light fitting, on the annex ceiling, near the veranda door.

So why was it important that I included this flickering light in my original notes? It may have been the case that this young man had a photosensitive reaction to the flickering light. His next task was to note the state of the shoelaces on the young man's footwear; if they were loose, he needed to know did staff open them, or were they untied prior to medical assistance being rendered.

The officer asked me if I would like to accompany him to check the laces, but I respectfully declined. At this stage in my life, I had gazed upon death too many times.

While he was away checking the footwear, I got a member of staff to arrange for someone from the hospital maintenance department to attend the scene. I needed to have the broken pane of glass removed from its frame and suitably packaged.

The police officer returned, and I told him that the glass was being removed, and he needed to seize it, as the coroner could ask to see it. I knew that the scene was in safe hands, so I signed out and returned to the office.

Here was a family looking forward to Christmas when tragedy struck. Life, as they knew it, would be changed forever as I too was to find out on Christmas Day 1998. Every Christmas Eve, before going to bed, I have a quiet moment in memory of this young man. Sorry, but I am keeping my personal tragedy private.

Some years later I attended a burglary scene at a church in Belfast. The church was less than a mile from the scene of this tragic accident. Entry had been gained by forcing a side door. Once inside, the burglar tried to force entry to an office, by striking a Georgian style wired glass pane with a fire extinguisher. The glass cracked but the wire mesh held.

I felt a tap on my shoulder from the key holder, who asked me if I was OK, and this broke my gaze. I did not realise it, but I had been deep in thought, staring at the broken glass pane. The burglary scene had provoked an immediate flashback to the accidental death of that young man.

My daughter phoned me, recently, asking me if I had attended a scene in a hospital where a young man had died while visiting his father. I asked her where she was and why she wanted to know this.

It turned out she was visiting a friend in hospital, and she was standing looking at a portrait, on a wall outside the ward, of a young boy who passed away while visiting his father.

I never knew that this image existed, but it was confirmed when she told me his name. The next thing I heard was my daughter's voice asking me if I was still there. My mind had been immersed in that Christmas Eve for a moment.
I told her that I was present and of course she wanted to know the tragic circumstances. I said nothing about the incident, but I wished her friend a speedy recovery.

The next incident took place in late summer. It was ten o'clock, with only an hour of my shift left. The day had been busy but thankfully uneventful and I was looking forward to getting home when the office phone rang, and my pager bleeped. Police needed me to attend the scene of an alleged suicide, on a railway track, near the town of Antrim.

It was nearing eleven when I parked the scenes of crime car on a nearby country road, from where I could see numerous torch lights, flickering like fireflies, in the distance. It was one of those pitch-black, late summer evenings where the air was still and quite warm. I lifted a large scene torch from the car and lit my path as I walked, across fields, towards the scene. The train track was bordered by hedge rows and trees on both sides and the only lighting was handheld. I logged into the scene, where a detective briefed me.

A young man had decided to take his own life. In this case it was suicide by train.
I suggested that he was a local man, who knew the train times and this remote location. However, my theory was not unanimously accepted, so I explained my thought process, to the sceptics, in simpler terms.

Who would arrive at this isolated location, at this time of night, then lie down on the train track in the hope that a train would be passing to run over their body. The sceptics went a little quiet after that. While I was waiting for the doctor to pronounce life extinct, and for photography personnel to attend, I introduced myself to the train driver. He, as you can imagine, was in a complete state of shock. I told him that I would get the doctor to speak with him as soon as he arrived.

The driver insisted that he was fine, but I could see that he was far from it. I checked the train for body parts, from front to rear, with negative results.

So here I was, beside a train track, in the middle of nowhere, with a young man's remains at various locations, inadequate lighting and time of the essence, as I needed to get the train driver and train released.

I walked over to the detective and asked him to organise 'Night Sun' to attend.
This request was at first declined, by someone sitting at a desk far away, but a few choice words from me and it was sorted.

Did you ever find yourself in a situation where you feel as if your need to extract your teeth, to get you noticed and your views across? A short time after my request we could hear the army helicopter in the distance. Minutes later the helicopter approached the scene, the pilot hovered it at a suitable height, and within seconds the entire scene was bathed in an arc of bright light. The beam from this intense light framed the area. It was like a scene from a slasher movie; but this was no movie. It was stark reality, laid bare, in all its horror. I examined the extremities of his remains for signs of restraints and this proved negative. I also searched the scene for drugs and discarded cans or bottles of alcoholic drinks. The scene was photographed, the doctor talked with the train driver, and then the train was released.

The police should have arranged for another driver, at an earlier stage in the investigation, to drive the train back to the station. However, the driver insisted that he would drive the train back. I do not know if I could have done what he did, having been subjected to such trauma and reliving it all, in the driver's cab, as he returned to the station. Thankfully, there were no passengers on the train that evening.

The only piece of his body still outstanding was his head. I widened the search area from where I had located the approximate first point of impact and I found what I was searching for in a surprisingly distant location. Due to the impact on his neck and the shape of a human head, this piece of his anatomy must have launched into the air before rolling down the railway embankment, ending its journey in deep grass below a pine tree.

His head had made a track in the grass. As I shone the torch at its final resting place his eyes were staring up at me. Before I packaged his head I looked directly at his eyes and paused for a moment of silence as a mark of respect. I had further time for reflection as I carried his head back up the embankment and placed it gently beside his body.

I checked again that we had all this young man's remains; police officers, suitable attired, placed them in a body bag and removed them from the scene for postmortem examination. The scene was searched again and nothing of an evidential nature was found. 'Night Sun' remained until the scene was closed.

Before leaving, I reminded the detective to contact the army and thank them for providing the light that we so needed.

I cannot imagine what this young man was feeling as he lay across the train tracks, waiting for the train to carry out his wish.

His arm, which was lying in the grass beside the track, was tattooed with his name.

Of all the carnage on view that night, it is this image and the image of his face that have remained with me to this day. The post-mortem results confirmed his death as suicide by train.

The following evening, I returned home, from work, to find that my wife had cooked me one of my favourite meals: bacon ribs, cabbage, and potatoes. The ribs were a non-starter, but I knew I needed to explain why, and I did, minus the graphic detail, of course. The cabbage and potatoes were not wasted. Our dogs enjoyed them.

I recently telephoned a gentleman to arrange a meeting with him and the place we eventually agreed to meet reactivated a memory of a scene that I had examined in this same County Antrim hotel. Some would say that his choice of location was coincidental, but I would disagree. We could have chosen another location.

The memory, which I thought had been well buried, was brought to the fore once more. This was yet another tragic scene where a young man ended his life.

I could have changed the venue when it was mentioned. But sometimes you must confront your demons for fear of them taking over.

I was asleep when my pager went off. Police required my presence at a scene of alleged suicide in a County Antrim hotel. Having been briefed by police at the scene, I accompanied an officer to a first-floor bedroom. Life had been pronounced extinct, and the deceased's body had been removed from the scene, prior to my arrival. From a scene examination perspective, I would have preferred it if police had left the scene intact, once there was no sign of life.

So, what had occurred that would make a young man decide that life was not worth living anymore? He had argued with his fiancée, who had left the party they were attending and gone to bed. Police were informed that this had been a substantial argument.

Some time passed when he decided to go to their room. At this point his fiancé was not aware that he was in the room. Some hours passed; she awoke to use the toilet, and it was then that she saw his lifeless body in the wardrobe.

He had removed his belt, placed it over the clothes rail in the wardrobe and buckled it, thus forming a noose. With the belt in place, he positioned his weight forward. This action closed his airway, resulting in his death. Why was I called out to this tragic scene when police believed that this was a case of suicide?

In all cases of suicide, I am there to make sure that there is no sign of foul play and that all was done that needed to be done, prior to the postmortem. His body and belt were not at the scene. So, what more was there for me to do?

I measured the height between the clothes rail and the floor of the wardrobe. I examined the construction of the clothes rail and how it was mounted. The rail looked very sturdy, so I tested its strength by trying to pull it from its mounting brackets. It did not budge.

This young man was quite tall so to have his airway obstructed he would have needed to position his legs straight out and directly to the rear while leaning forward onto his belt.

It is possible that he tested the strength of the clothes rail. Or on the other hand he may have believed that it would give way and the noise of him falling free would be sufficient to wake his fiancée. One will never know.

If only he had woken her up to sort things out. I passed the information I had gathered to the officer in charge; the coroner might ask questions in connection with my measurements. I signed out of the log and went back to the office, where I had a cup to tea and reflected on how a few harsh words could result in the death of this young man. Another life lost to the power of words and the future altered forever.

What was it that made an octogenarian take his own life? I was on duty when local police asked me to attend the scene of a suspected suicide in Belfast.

As I was walking through the entrance hall of this red brick terraced house a young police officer introduced herself and asked me to step outside so that she could brief me on what had taken place.

I knew straight away that this scene was in capable hands. Armed with the necessary information I went back into the house and ushered everyone in the hallway into the downstairs back room and closed the door.

I then asked the other police officer if he would sit in the front room with the wife of the deceased and close the door behind him. I looked at the body and shut my eyes inwardly sounding my usual two words, "God bless."

The body of a fully clothed elderly man was stretched out on the stairs, face upwards. On closer inspection of his throat, directly below his chin, I could see a red abrasion and the weave of fibres, consistent with a rope ligature, impressed into his skin.

Police had discreetly searched the house and had asked his wife if she knew where the rope was, but she just stared at the television. The police had contacted family, and the doctor had already attended to pronounce life extinct.

I inspected the newel post at the top of the stairs and the area directly below it. This newel post showed signs of fresh damage and several small paint flakes were visible on the stair carpet directly below the post.

I was satisfied that a rope had been anchored on the newel post and that the gentleman had tied the other end around his neck and, by sliding down the stairs, he had taken his own life. His feet were almost touching the hall wall.

But where was the rope?

I entered the front downstairs room and asked the police officer to join his colleague in the hall. I sat down beside this lady, who did not avert her gaze from the television. I could see that she was clearly in shock.
A well-known and long running soap opera, based in Manchester, was on the television, so I just sat in silence until the commercial break. When the ads came on, I asked her if she was a fan of this show; she just looked straight ahead.

I then asked her if she remembered two of the original actors and this got an immediate response. We talked a little more and I brought the matter of the missing rope into the conversation. She told me that it was in the blanket box in the main bedroom. Police recovered a blue coloured nylon rope, inside a plastic shopping bag, in the blanket box that lay on the floor at the bottom of the bed.

I explained to the investigating officer that she had hidden the rope out of shame; she did not want anyone to know that her husband had taken his own life. Prior to leaving I passed on my condolences. The past mortem results confirmed that it was a suicide.

It was never established why he had taken the decision to end his life. So how did I know about this English soap opera? Good old granny was looking down and came to my rescue. My granny was a fan of this soap opera and as a young boy I had been press-ganged into watching it with her on occasions. I never became a fan.

The next tragedy took place in a family home in County Antrim. It was just another routine day for this family, or so it would appear. The parents left for work and the children went to school. This is a familiar pattern in many households.

However, this pattern was about to be broken in the most tragic of circumstances.
The family dynamic, as you know, is extremely complex; I cannot pretend to know what occurred, prior to this tragic event taking place. And it is not my place to speculate.

Police requested my presence at the scene of an alleged suicide. I arrived at this semi-detached house and the investigating officer briefed me outside the front door of the property.

The body of a male was in the main bedroom upstairs and life had been pronounced extinct by an FMO.

The lady of the house returned home to find her husband dead on the bedroom floor.

The deceased was fully dressed, lying face up, on the bedroom floor. He had taken a large carving knife from the kitchen, walked upstairs into the main bedroom, lay down on the floor and forced the blade into his chest.

There was no sign of a struggle, and the only visible sign of blood was a slight seepage into his clothing from a single wound. I found out later why he decided that life was no longer worth living.

This gentleman had lost his job, several months earlier, but he would get up each morning and leave for work as if everything were normal. It obviously got to the stage where he could no longer carry on with the pretence, so he ended his life, rather than tell his wife the truth.

The following scene involved death by means of prescription drugs. I do not know if I would have the courage to do what this lady did. Then again, I was not in her shoes. Driven to extremes, people can act in extraordinary ways and sometimes out of necessity when faced with the inevitable.

A lady contacted police as she had not heard from her friend for a couple of days, despite several telephone calls. Police arrived at a large, detached house in South Belfast. There was no sign of a forced entry but when a police officer peered through a kitchen window at the rear of the property, he noticed the body of a lady on the kitchen floor.

The officers forced an entry and quickly established that the lady was dead. A Force Medical Officer attended and pronounced life extinct. The investigating officer briefed me in the living room, and I commenced my examination of the scene.

As I walked along the hall, in the direction of the kitchen, I stopped for a moment to look at a photograph of a lady in a nursing uniform, on the hall wall. She looked about the same age as my mother, who was a district midwife at the time.

Despite having attended many scenes of this nature I would always be a little apprehensive, as I was about to gaze upon death once more.

I stood in the hall for a while and scanned the room. This quiet time allowed me to focus. The deceased was lying face up on the kitchen floor, wearing pyjamas and a dressing gown. It was the lady from the photograph.

On the kitchen table, to my left, was a glass which contained a small amount of clear liquid and beside this glass there was a small mound of empty packaging, which had contained prescription tablets.

The kitchen chairs were all neatly in place, around the table, bar one. There were a few loose tablets on the table and some on the kitchen floor. I checked the remaining liquid in the glass; it was water, and the tablet packaging contained the name of the deceased.

Why had she made a conscious decision to consume a cocktail of prescription drugs to end her life? Her decision, as I was to discover later, was taken because of a medical diagnosis that she had received. This lady, who lived alone, had been treated for cancer and survived; but the cancer returned years later, and her diagnosis was life limiting.

Here was a nurse who had, no doubt, witnessed death many times in her professional life, deciding to leave this world on her own terms rather than letting nature take its course. I admired her for such courage. Others may think the opposite.

This next case is yet another tragic occurrence that took place due to emotionally complex family circumstances.
A gentleman telephoned police to say that he had called at his son's home and found his son lying dead in the rear of the company van.
The house where the death occurred was on the outskirts of Belfast and as I entered the drive, a middle-aged gentleman approached the car and signalled me to drive to the rear of the property. Ambulance personnel had attended and confirmed that a young man was in the back of the van and there was no sign of life. I arranged for a Force Medical Officer to attend to confirm life extinct. While waiting for the FMO I accompanied the gentleman into the house, where he introduced me to his wife, who was seated at a kitchen table. This large detached secluded property was hidden from the

main road and bordered on three sides by tall trees leading to open fields.

I noticed several savings books, arranged in a neat row on the table. This couple told me why their son had taken his own life. So why had he done it?
Their son was married with two children, and he had told his parents that his wife was having an affair; when he confronted her, she took the children, left the family home, and had not returned.

At this point his mother lifted the savings books and opened them to reveal a substantial amount of money in the accounts. They were truly angry, stating that all this money and the property, along with a share in the family business, would go to her. I could only empathise with their loss. You need to be a good listener when you are faced with such a tragic scenario. It was time for me to examine the scene. I attended the van with the FMO and when he had left, I asked the parents to remain in the house, while I carried out my examination.
The gentleman had removed two photo frames from the house, which contained photographs of his children, and placed them in the rear of his van. After taping a length of

garden hose to the exhaust he placed the open end of the hose in the rear of the van, started the van, climbed into the rear, and closed the van doors. He was found in the foetal position, in the rear of the van, by his parents. The last faces he saw were those of his two young children.

While I was sitting at my desk in Tennent Street RUC Station, a Detective Sergeant walked in and asked me if I could go with him to a property in West Belfast, to investigate an alleged suicide.
He briefed me on the way to the scene with regards to this incident. Police had received a call from a man who reported that his wife had committed suicide, and her body was lying in the front garden.

At this point in the investigation the lady's remains had already been removed and were at the Belfast City Mortuary, awaiting a postmortem. The Detective Sergeant had spoken to the husband and become suspicious about the man's version of events. His gut instinct was telling him that something did not add up.

My priority was to phone the mortuary staff. Thankfully, the postmortem had not started so I explained the situation and put the examination on hold.

I asked the DS to contact the police officer who attended the scene, when the body was in the garden, and get him to meet me at the location ASAP. I needed to know the exact position of the body, as this would be of vital importance in my scene examination.

Armed with this information about the body, I entered this first floor flat with the D/Sgt, who pointed to an open living room window. The husband of the deceased had told the police that he saw his wife open this window and jump out, which resulted in her death.

The living room window frame was constructed of metal, with two solid glass panes along its entire width and up to my waist level. The two side widows, directly above these solid glass panes, were separated by a solid glass pane between them.

To open these side windows, one had to hold a central latch and push outwards. The window in question was on the right, as one looked out. I established that this window did not extend fully outwards without considerable effort and even then, it did not extend out as far as its twin, to my left.

Armed with this information we returned to Tennent Street, RUC Station. I needed a test dummy so that I could carry out some experiments at the scene. I contacted a forensic scientist, a specialist in this type of work, and he met me at the scene, with his orange-coloured companion.

I contacted the mortuary and obtained information about the woman's weight and height, the injuries that she had sustained and lastly what she was wearing. So why did I need to know all this? It would be vital for us to make our tests as realistic as possible.

We filled our orange-coloured flexible friend with sand so that it was the same weight as the deceased, allowing for clothing. This test dummy was the same height as the deceased. So, we were ready to begin.

We spent hours at the scene, where we tried numerous times to replicate what had occurred, according to her husband's story. After an exhaustive series of tests we concluded that this was not a suicide.

Our hypothesis was that this lady had been leaning out the window when someone approached from behind, grabbed her legs and tumbled her out to her death. Despite our best efforts we could not disprove this hypothesis.

I passed this information onto the Detective Sergeant. A few hours later he called to tell me that her husband had confessed to killing his wife once he was made aware of the results of our scene examination.

I contacted the duty scientist to give him the good news and I thanked him for providing his expertise. This was reported as a suicide, but it turned out to be the complete opposite.

Thanks to the sharp observations and listening skills of this seasoned Detective Sergeant, a confession of murder was speedily obtained.

Attempting to find a balance between your professional life, some personal time and family life, coupled with the pressures of day-to-day living, can be a challenge for most people.

The following scene was not only harrowing, in so many ways, it also involved the loss of a talent that gave others the gift of a better life.

It was a warm summer afternoon when I received a message, on my pager, to attend the scene of an alleged suicide, in a residential room on the grounds of a Belfast hospital. These residential units were occupied by medical staff attached to the hospital. My partner and I had just examined a burglary scene nearby and I informed Belfast Regional Control that I would be there directly.

As I was parking the SOCO car I noticed a crowd of people to my right, standing outside a small single-story building, and a local detective heading towards the car, post-haste. The area was cordoned off and a scene log was visible in the hands of a local police officer. I remained by the car while the detective briefed me with regards to what had taken place, thus far.

A young surgeon had been paged several times, as his skills were needed in theatre, but he had not replied. Staff searched the hospital and eventually found his lifeless body, sitting in an upright position on the bed, in his residential flat within the hospital grounds. Life had been pronounced extinct, and a police photographer and mapper were on their way.

My partner and I suited up, went through the usual documentary routine, and entered the scene. What had occurred for this young surgeon to conclude that his life was not worth living?

It is extremely important, at all scenes, to observe your surroundings, in all directions, prior to commencing an examination. It can be the case that an item needs to be recovered extremely quickly due to its perishable nature. I have been to scenes where police responders have recovered or protected items, prior to my arrival, for which I commended them, both orally and in writing, for such due diligence. Here is a little information for you; always remember to look up if the location warrants it.

Standing at the threshold of the bedroom door, I scanned the entire contents of the small room. There was no visible sign of a struggle having taken place. On the bed, to my right, was the body of this young man and an empty syringe. I also noticed a piece of A4-sized paper, on a dressing table, directly in front of me, with something underneath it. What was making it bulge?

On closer inspection I could see that this was a handwritten letter, in a foreign script, the contents of which might reveal why this young man took his own life. My preliminary observation over, and having touched nothing, I walked out of the room to await the arrival of my colleagues from photography and mapping, so that they could capture and record everything within the scene prior to my examination.

My partner and I had been at the scene for quite a while, waiting for photography and mapping units to attend, when the detective came to the front door and asked us to walk out of the property; this was an order from a Senior Investigating Officer.

This SIO was on his way and had instructed that no one was to enter the scene until he arrived. We had met him at previous major scenes, so we were very much aware of his skill set. We also knew that he was destined for this lofty rank.

I informed the detective that we would be remaining in the property awaiting other experts and that I would take responsibility. Time was of the essence due to the heat outside and inside the building. The crowd outside the property had doubled in numbers and our colleagues had just arrived. My patience by now was wearing thin.

I looked at the crowd and noticed some people, whom I believed were of the same ethnic origin as the deceased, so getting the contents of the letter translated, in confidence, would not be an issue, once it had been photographed, mapped, and packaged as evidence.

The SIO arrived and quizzed the detective as to why we were in the scene followed by a verbal onslaught on both my partner and me. This berating, in front of an audience, was short but not sweet. How unprofessional, condescending, and rude.

The outburst reminded me, once again of Plato, the learned Athenian philosopher, who got it spot on when he said, 'The untrained mind keeps up a running commentary, labelling everything, judging everything. Best to ignore that commentary. Do not argue or resist, just ignore it. Deprived of attention and interest, this voice gets quieter and quieter and eventually just shuts up.'

We were long enough in the tooth to let it go in one ear and out the other. We nodded dutifully, in unison, rather than acknowledge an ill-timed, discourteous rant.

Somewhere in the middle of his tiresome tirade, he ordered me to get him a crime scene suit from the car; I knew that I did not have one that would fit properly. To do this, I had to leave the scene. I complied reluctantly and handed over the suit, with the proviso that it would not fit. As soon as he donned it, the suit was forensically compromised due to several splits. Time was marching on, and we needed to get on with our examination.

This young man's body was still at the scene and people were watching while a square peg was trying to fit into a round hole. I informed the SIO that everything was as I found it and that the scene needed to be photographed and mapped before anything could be moved. Still suited and booted, we waited in the narrow entrance hall as the born leader entered the bedroom. The first thing he lifted was the letter; perhaps he understood its contents. When he moved the letter, he dislodged the item that had been making the letter bulge.

It was a second syringe, filled with a yellowish coloured liquid. With its paper blanket removed, the syringe fell onto the floor of the bedroom where, upon impact, it spurted some of its contents onto the floor.

My partner and I looked at each other and it did not require the presence of a clairvoyant to interpret our thoughts. In a matter of minutes and with no further distraction I was back in charge of the scene.

Photography and mapping completed their task and then I finally got to commence my examination, ably assisted by my partner. I entered the bedroom on my own, stood beside this young man's body, closed my eyes, and reflected, in silence, on yet another tragic loss of life.

The contents of the letter, once they were translated, described private family circumstances, with which he could not reconcile. Being in the medical profession afforded him access to drugs and, using his medial knowledge, he self-administered a lethal dose of medication that stopped his heart.

I wondered why he needed a second syringe. Perhaps he thought that he needed this amount of medication to carry out the grim task but, when the time came, he realised that one syringe would suffice.

This next case opened an old memory that has been locked away for more than forty years.

Both incidents involved road traffic accidents, and both ended in the loss of life. I had buried a memory of the death of my sister's friend, who lost his life when crossing the road outside the school where he had been a pupil.
This young man had safely crossed to the centre of the road, but someone called him back. He turned to his left, to look behind him, and in turning he stepped into the path of a car in the lane that he had just crossed. His back was facing the oncoming car at the time of impact, and that led to his premature death at the age of fifteen.

Late one evening, I was standing on the Upper Newtownards Road, at the scene of a fatal road traffic accident, involving a lorry and a pedestrian, when that old memory was triggered. By this time in my career, I had dealt with several fatal road traffic accidents. Funny that this particular incident should drag up old memories.

In this case a gentleman had been crossing the road when, for whatever reason, he turned back and into the path of a lorry, which resulted in his death. These two incidents were many years apart but perhaps my brain was making a comparison with what it perceived as common factors in both cases: crossing a road, male pedestrians, vehicles involved and a decision to turn back while crossing. Who knows?

The role of a CSI, at this type of incident, is to aid the investigating police officer so that everything has been photographed, mapped, and examined. Sometimes a forensic scientist needs to attend such scenes but that is only in cases where his or her specialism is required.

There are numerous matters to consider at a scene such as this one: street lighting, skid marks, the driver's view, if the lorry is fitted with a tachograph, the point of impact between the pedestrian and the lorry, there may be alcohol involved, the mechanical condition of the lorry (this is examined at a later date) and one needs to recover debris of interest from the road surface, if there is any.

The investigating officer will carry out a full investigation and prepare a case file. In most cases of this nature, I am not informed of the full circumstances of events unless the coroner requires my presence at an inquest, where the history of events is discussed for all present to hear.

Over the years I have been contacted by a few investigating officers, as a professional courtesy, to inform me of the outcome of their cases. However, the tragic events of this case were to be relayed to me in a conversation which I once again put under the heading of, 'my meant to be moments.'

A few days later I was made aware of what had occurred prior to this man losing his life. I was sitting in my kitchen when my front doorbell sounded. I opened the door to greet my friend and neighbour. I could see that she was distressed, and her voice confirmed this when she spoke. As we walked towards the kitchen, she asked me if I had been to the scene of a fatal road accident, where a gentleman had been struck by a lorry.

138

I sat her down at the table and, while I was making her a cup of tea, I told her that I had been at the scene, but I could not discuss the details of the case. She respected my position. However, I could see that she needed to talk about the accident, so I put on my active listening hat as she laid bare her inner thoughts. My neighbour was originally from London and the deceased had been a close friend.

Here is what she told me.

Her friend had recently moved to Northern Ireland, from London to be around a group of friends he had grown up with, as they were now living in County Down.

On the morning in question, he took his close friend's children to school in their family car. Having left the children to school he set off on the return journey. However, not being familiar with the roads, he took a wrong turn, crashed the car into a post and sustained an impact injury to his head.

As a result of the injury, he was taken to hospital, where he asked a member of staff to phone his friend (my neighbour), so that she would collect the children from school.

139

My neighbour collected the children, left them home and then phoned a friend, who worked at the hospital, asking her to enquire about his condition. This friend made inquiries, but no one could locate him. Police searched the hospital grounds and the surrounding area but did not find him.

While in casualty awaiting assessment, he answered the phone at the doctors' station and introduced himself to the caller before a member of staff was able to interrupt. Sometime later and for a reason only known to himself, he walked out of the hospital.

Did the earlier accident cause some form of delirium? One will never know. This gentleman left his roots to be close to his boyhood friends, but circumstance dealt him a fatal blow. My neighbour still misses him.

There are not enough adjectives in the English language to describe the tragedy and life altering events contained within these scenes. It is cases like these that eat into your mind and occupy their own unique space on what I term the 'shelf of why.' Let me leave you with an image of what happens inside my head when I recall these cases.

Do you know what a spiralizer is?

The budding chefs out there will know. A spiralizer is a small electrical appliance that turns fresh vegetables into a tangled mass of spirals; the more you feed the machine the larger the mass becomes and the more tangled it becomes.

I need to lie down now to try to unravel the tangled mass of thoughts within my brain.

Goodnight for now.

Stonyford is a small village in County Antrim, approximately five miles north of Lisburn. In September 1993, a colleague and I were in the SOCO office of Tennent Street RUC Station when the phone rang. There had been a shooting in Stonyford, resulting in the death of a local man, Sean McGovern. The IRA had issued a warning to all hauliers who delivered materials to the security forces in Northern Ireland to stop this practise or they would become legitimate targets. What kind of person makes a statement like this? I cannot understand how such actions would advance their cause and equally why some people would fund them. The only thing these cowards left was a legacy of pain and loss that would never be forgotten or forgiven.

In September 1993 three young boys, aged eight, five and three stood in their driveway looking at the dead body of their father. What a heart-piercing sight. Mr McGovern had been a hard-working member of this rural community and his wife, who was a nurse at the time, was expecting their fourth child.

My colleague and I checked that we had all the necessary equipment on board before heading to the scene. During the drive, with my brain in fight mode, a thought came to mind. It is fascinating how a random thought enters the brain and forces you to change tack when you are concentrating on something else.

The area where I was heading to was where my mum had begun her career as a district midwife, cycling around the country lanes carrying out home deliveries, if the circumstances were favourable. I shook my head to clear it and got back to the task at hand. It was a dark and clear night. I parked the car on raised ground that overlooked and provided an unobstructed view of the scene, some seventy meters away. From this vantage point I could see everything. Ahead and to the left there was a bungalow, bathed in light. The spotlights, at the front of the property, highlighted the front driveway and garden area. There was a lorry parked on the road, to my right. The position of this lorry would have provided the culprits with a clear line of sight.

On the front driveway, between the front door and the entrance gates, there was a body almost covered in a blanket. I also noticed someone walking near the attached garage. At this stage life had been pronounced extinct.
I could see that police had the cordon tape in place; it was time to speak with the scene log officer. We introduced ourselves before donning our scene suits.

The log officer had been instructed by the Detective Inspector that no one was to enter the scene, at present, so we returned to the car and waited. We were waiting for about thirty minutes when there was a knock on the car window. It was the head of CID, Belfast. He wanted to know why we were sitting in the car, and I told him that we were under instruction from the DI. He noticed the same person that we had seen earlier inside the cordon; it was the DI. We were logged into the scene a few minutes later with the DI still doing whatever he had to do.

I was there to examine the main scene while my colleague was there to examine the lorry. So why did I not examine this scene in its entirety, with my colleague assisting? After all, everything was in close proximity. This approach was taken to eliminate cross contamination of potential evidence. The lorry and the murder scene were connected; but for forensic examination purposes they were separate.

Mr McGovern had seen his friend's lorry arrive and so he went over to see why he was there. He expected to see his friend, but he was cut down in a hail of bullets.
While I was working through the scene in the direction of Mr McGovern's body, I heard the screaming of two ladies; I looked up to see them walking towards me. One of the ladies was Mrs McGovern and the other, I think, was Mr McGovern's mother.
They were both asked to remain outside the inner cordon, but they wanted to see him. At this point I had examined everywhere apart from the body, so I walked over and broke protocol. I told them that they could come with me, but they could not touch the body. As we approached, their grief was palpable. I was ready should anyone collapse. Standing over the body, Mrs McGovern asked if she could see Sean, who

was still under the blanket provided by the ambulance service.

I changed my gloves and lifted the blanket, which revealed the side of his face and shoulders. Both ladies knelt, tears streaming down their faces. I had an arm around each of them when Mrs McGovern thanked me for making this happen. I had just placed the blanket back over his body when Mrs McGovern told me that her husband had a gun, which he carried everywhere. I thanked her for that information.

Mrs McGovern stood nearby as I searched his body, and I found the holstered handgun below his leather jacket. The ladies left, distraught, and I carried on with my examination. I removed the handgun and made it safe before packaging it.

I am in no doubt that Mr McGovern was aware of the terrorist threat to hauliers in his position. However, he did not give in to this threat; like many before him, he carried on making his deliveries to support his family. I recognise the inner strength and conviction that he clearly possessed; some of you may not.

To me Sean McGovern, John Haldane, and John McMaster, to name but a few, are local heroes.

All being well the McGovern boys would now be grown men aged; 39, 36, and 34. I wonder if their mum gave birth to a girl or another boy. I hope that the passage of time has allowed them to cope, but they will never forget.

Norman Truesdale was thirty-nine when two gunmen entered his grocery shop, on the Oldpark Road, Belfast, and shot him dead. The location of this murder is less than a mile from Tennent Street RUC. His family, at the time, said that Norman was not involved with paramilitaries. However, several years later his brother acknowledged that he believed Norman had taken part in an attack on a local bookmaker, where three people were killed. A young boy was in the shop when the gunmen entered to take their revenge, and he saw and heard everything.

So, what part did I play in the investigation of this murder? I was at my desk when the phone rang. It was the same detective who ate part of my lunch the last time he was in the office. He told me that there had been a shooting in a grocery shop on the Oldpark Road and the owner was dead at the scene.

I thought 'here we go again, another killing' but his request was for me to attend the holding centre at Castlereagh RUC station and examine a suspect. However, he needed me to meet him in the CID office of Antrim Road RUC station.

The murder had been recorded on the shop's CCTV, and he had a copy. He wanted me to view the killing prior to dealing with the gunman. I was still on the phone with him, and we had a brief discussion about the contents of the disk. After hearing what he said I explained that I did not need to see the video; it would not assist me in my examination of the suspect.

He asked me to wait on the line and the next voice I heard was my old golf chum, the Detective Chief, who told me, in as calm a voice as possible, 'get your fucking arse over here and take a look at this.' I walked into the CID office fifteen minutes later.

I did not attend as the result of being ordered. I attended out of respect for the rank and the eloquent request from my golfing chum.

I walked over to the Chief and smiled. 'I didn't think you used vulgar words.' That, of course, provoked more vulgar words, as he directed me to my seat for the viewing. I was injecting a little dark humour for what my eyes were about to receive.

Most movies that we view today are in colour. In this case the scene was in black and white and, having viewed the sickening content, it reminded me of the old gangster movies set in Chicago; but this was real life. So, did I need to see it? No, I did not. The Scenes of Crime officer attending the scene needed to see it. Then the penny dropped. My golf chum and the detectives present needed some forensic input on what had taken place, which I duly provided.

I had sleepless nights because of this viewing, and I often thought about the young boy who witnessed the shooting, with the noise of gunfire and the last spoken words of Norman Truesdale ringing in his ears. The second gunman was never caught and the suspect that I dealt with was given a life sentence. Like many others he was given a get out of jail card as he became a beneficiary of the Good Friday Agreement.

## Who murdered Adrian Lamph?

This was another cold case murder that I reviewed while I was a civilian member of the Retrospective Murder Review Unit.

On 21 April 1998, a gunman cycled up to Adrian and shot him dead, while he was standing at the Fair Green Amenity Centre in Portadown. Adrian, a law-abiding member of the Catholic community, worked at this centre at the time of his death. He was a father of one, earning an honest living to provide for his family. His son was only one year old.

Muriel Gibson was jailed for eight years for a string of offences. One of them was impeding the arrest and prosecution of the killers of Adrian Lamph; she was also convicted of membership of the Loyalist Volunteer Force, possessing firearms, detonators, and pipe-bombs. She never divulged the name of the killer who carried out this purely sectarian murder.

There was considerable speculation circulating, as to who the gunman was. However, as you know speculation means nothing. The police need conclusive evidence so they can proceed with a prosecution. In some cases, a strong chain of circumstantial evidence will suffice.

I commenced this review in the same manner as all my previous cold case reviews. My first port of call was to get my hands on the most recent police review of the case. This review was carried out by senior officers attached to the Serious Crime Review Team, based in Belfast. I opened this file and read it from start to finish. It concluded that all was done that could be done; but if any new information were to become available this would be acted upon immediately.

I always start off with the hope that I will find something to progress a case. However, the 'dog of doubt' is always clinging on in the background. It takes weeks to review this type of case file. I would find an avenue of enquiry, arrange to meet the scientist, discuss the issue and then it is onto the next avenue.

There are also a considerable number of dead ends. So, did I find something of interest? I think I did, but perhaps not. However, I thought that it was worth a scientist taking another look.

I was not privy to the outcome of my review, that I forwarded to the Senior Investigation Officer, as my employment at RMRU ended a short time later. What I had found may have been something and yet again nothing.

In any case, Mr Lamph's murder remained unresolved during my tenure.

Who was Peter McTasney?

Peter was a 26-year-old catholic gentleman. He was a voluntary worker and family man who devoted his free time for the betterment of his local community and beyond.

Peter was standing in the living room of his, Bawnmore Park, home when he was murdered. His 3-year-old daughter was by his side, and she sustained a wound to her face.

Bawnmore, an estate on the outskirts of Belfast, has had its share of serious crime over the years.

The living room light was on, and the blinds were pulled back so this, unfortunately, provided the gunman with an easy target. Peter stood no chance of escaping.

The gunman fired through the living room window. This first bullet struck Peter and at the same time a second offender, wielding a sledgehammer, smashed open the front door followed by the same gunman who discharged his weapon again fatally wounding Peter. This was yet another senseless sectarian murder that achieved absolutely nothing.

The ripple effect left behind in the aftermath of such heinous crimes is everlasting. Violence perpetuates violence, of that there is no doubt.

This was a scene that needed to be secured due to its location. I based myself, along with my photography and mapping colleagues, at Newtownabbey RUC station, waiting to be trucked to the scene. This police station is around two miles from Bawnmore.

A substantial crowd greeted us when we arrived and as I stepped out of the armoured police car a fight broke out between residents and police officers. We were escorted through the crowd to the house. Peter's body had already been removed from the scene. I signed into the scene log and properly attired I began my examination, while my two colleagues did what they had to do, under my instruction.

So, what would you expect to recover from this scene?

I took glass samples from the living room window as glass not only enters the property but also deflects back in the direction of the gun man.

If someone is arrested promptly then small fragments of this glass may be lodged in their clothing, hair, and footwear. The vehicle used in this crime may also contain glass, from the scene, through trace contact between the culprits and the interior surfaces of the vehicle.

I examined the front door, and tape lifted its surface in case there were fibres present that were not visible to the human eye.

My next task was to recover blood and bullets. The bullets had penetrated the leather suite and lodged in the internal wooden frame. While standing in the living room I could see and hear a running battle between residents and police. I needed to wrap this scene up before matters escalated.

Peter had been murdered, I was there to recover potential evidence, my police colleagues were being assaulted, reinforcements were on the way and the local mob was getting out of control. A scenario like this has all the ingredients to develop into a threat to life.

I took hold of my carpet style knife and removed the leather from the suite, post-haste, to access the bullets wedged in the frame. A fingerprint examination of the scene proved negative for evidence.
Reinforcements had just arrived so with potential evidence in hand it was time to exit 'Dodge.' On the way to the vehicles, we were met with a hail of mixed debris and thankfully their aim was off.

Many police officers were battered and bruised, and one lost several teeth in the melee.

What a night! I still have the orange-coloured carpet knife to remind me of the horror and futility of what had taken place. Another innocent life cut short.

# Chapter 5

# Volume Crime and other Offences

A veritable catalogue of crime falls under this heading: burglary, theft, taking a vehicle without the owner's consent (TWOC), criminal damage and some assaults.

The term 'volume crime' in no way diminishes the fact that someone has been the victim of these offences; it is purely a category heading under which such crimes are placed. These crimes have a significant impact on the general community due to their sheer numbers and, in a lot of cases, police forces are playing catch up to deal with them.

Pleas for funding or resources come up against the same old carousel of jaded rhetoric: this costs money, that costs money, or insurance companies can pick up the bill. We need to see more police on our streets, and we need more permanent specialist units to deal with volume crime.

You hear and read about crime statistics and how certain police forces have done a splendid job because their volume crime rates are down by one or two percent. Some people are so engrossed in the good news that they forget about the human cost involved.

Burglary of a home is so much more that someone damaging and stealing your property. I wonder if anyone has data that would tell us about the psychological and physical impact that burglary has on those who have been victims of this crime and the subsequent cost of providing medical care.

A burglar enters your home, steals your possessions, and leaves behind anger, fear, shock, vulnerability, and panic for you to endure. For some people, the trauma of such an event can eventually develop into post-traumatic stress disorder, anxiety attacks and much more, as if the original insult was not enough.

I have examined many burglary scenes over the years, and I cannot remember any of those people that I caught, as a result of finding evidence at the scene, getting a punishment that would deter them from re-offending.

However, having said that, for some criminals, burglary is their chosen career, or their compulsion. In my experience, having an alarm system fitted is a good deterrent and having a panic switch beside your bed will make you feel less vulnerable.

I remember going to a scene where an elderly gentleman had a bell box fitted to the front eaves of his home and he was furious that a burglar had broken in, despite the obvious deterrent.

He had bought this item from a website, and, from a distance, it looked the part.

On closer inspection I could see that there was no light coming from it. It was only a plastic box with the appearance of a deterrent. It was not functional in any way.

The burglar was wise to the idea of fake alarms; he simply checked it over and broke in. The scene did not offer up any evidence. After a chat and a cup of tea the gentleman appeared less angry. I was in the area several weeks later and called in to see him. I could see that he had had a new alarm installed. He was delighted with the alarm, as it only cost a few hundred pounds, it was easy to work, and he had peace of mind. The answer to your thoughts is yes, I had another cup of tea while we talked, and I listened intently. He lived on his own and no doubt relished the company.

If you do not have an alarm fitted, please get one. Do I have one? Yes, I do, and it is also pet friendly. The burglar is always looking for an easy target but there are some burglars that thrive on a challenge.

Allow me to inform you how a career burglar, from Belfast, was caught after having committed, according to the detectives in charge of these cases, eighty burglaries of family homes.  In all of these crimes the occupants of the houses were asleep when he entered, and they were not aware of his presence inside their property. This information, along with other details, which I will outline, only became known to detectives when they had interviewed the injured parties, collated the methods of entry to the properties and assessed the locations of the crimes. This burglar was, unfortunately for police, very proficient at what he did best. He was as elusive as the Scarlet Pimpernel but with one main difference; he helped himself and not others. So how was such a scoundrel caught? I happily confess that 'scoundrel' was not the word I first thought of.

I had examined burglary scenes of homes in a particular area of North Down, which bore his modus operandi (a particular way of doing something), and at all these scenes nothing of evidential value was found; there were no fingerprints, DNA, fibres, hair, footwear impressions, or CCTV.

The burglar gained entry to these properties by using some kind of tool to access one of the locking cams of the multi-lock, which runs along the interior edge of most double-glazed doors.

By applying a gentle upward pressure on this cam, the other cams will move in unison and entry is gained. Some of the points of entry bore scuff marks from the tool used to force entry so I made casts of them, to see if the scuff marks were all similar — and they were. However, this was merely informative rather than evidential.

Once inside the property he would search for documents that had a date of birth on them, and he would take a door key. Why would he need a date of birth? Many people use their year of birth as their pin code to withdraw cash from an ATM. So now all he needed was a bank card.

Having obtained all three, he would go to the nearest cash MACHINE and, if luck were on his side, he would withdraw a small amount of money. With the cash in his pocket he returns to the property, puts the card back where he found it, locks the rear door using the key and leaves while the occupants are still asleep. He is now in possession of your house key.

This process was repeated many times, with multiple properties; large or tiny amounts of cash were withdrawn each time. His nest egg was becoming substantial.

The two detectives in charge of the case were relentless in their pursuit of our man but they could not catch a break. I accompanied them on several stakeouts, at ungodly hours of the night, in the affluent areas where this burglar plied his trade, with no success.

My shift pattern during this time was eight to four and four to midnight, so if I were on one of these stakeouts I would start around ten the next morning instead of eight. On one such morning I was telephoned at home, around nine o'clock, by one of the detectives; she wanted me to revisit a small number of burglary scenes, near each other. These scenes had been previously examined by colleagues with negative results for evidence. This detective just wanted a second opinion and so we meet in her office for a briefing.

This was my favourite CID office because, on arrival, I was always treated to a cup of tea with a scone or a pastry, and I passed the time in pleasant company.

Having been briefed and with tummy well fed I attended the burglary scenes in question. My re-examinations supported the findings my colleagues had produced. I was in no doubt that these scenes were all the work of the same stealth burglar. However, there was one scene that was very interesting.

I rang the front doorbell, and the door was answered by a lady in her dressing gown. I introduced myself; I could see that this lady was in a hurry, while she told me a brief story of events. I was left to carry on with my examination as she hurried away to get ready for an appointment.
A substantial amount of money had been stolen from her home and, to make matters worse, the insurance company would not honour her claim. They declined to reimburse her because the CSI report stated that a point of entry could not

be established; so, in the insurer's opinion, she had left the property insecure.

This lady was most irate, to say the least, because she was adamant that she had secured her home, as she usually did, but the insurers did not believe her. I examined the windows and doors for signs of damage and there was none. All the surfaces in question still bore signs of black fingerprint powder from the earlier examination. In this case the burglar had left the scene with the Motherload.

However, on the exterior surface of the rear UPVC door, just below the handle, there was a small area where the dirt had been smeared. On opening this door, I noticed a minute, 'V' shaped cut on the black coloured weather strip, adjacent to the door handle and in line with one of the cams that formed part of the door's multi-lock.

This piece of weatherstrip was so small that one could have missed it during an examination. It helps to have an eye like a travelling rat.

The corresponding piece of weather strip was lying on top of a layer of dust that covered the entire surface of the frame void below. I can hear you asking,
'Could this piece of weather strip have been there since the door was fitted?'

I like your theory but on close inspection of this small fragment I could see that its upper surface was void of dust. I had found the point of entry.

This burglary bore all the hallmarks of our stealth burglar. I was sitting at the breakfast bar, writing up my notes, when the lady walked in and asked me if I had found anything.

I confirmed that it was a burglary, and my scene report would reflect this. The lady then hugged me and asked me if I would like a cup of tea and a sandwich and, before I could respond, she asked me to listen to a phone call first. What could I say but 'OK.' The telephone conversation was with her bank manager, as the house insurance was through the bank.

I would like to repeat what was said but confidentially and data protection spring to mind, so I am afraid I will have to leave you guessing.

I could see that she was pumped with adrenalin at this news, so I thanked her but declined the offer of refreshments, as I needed to attend the next scene on my list.

Anyway, I could not eat so soon after having had breakfast in the local CID office. There is only so much refreshment a man can take.

I had not caught my burglar, but the result was a bonus for the owner of the house.

A few weeks passed with no sign of our suspect coming out of the shadows.

He was spending some of his ill-gotten gains. However, his crime spree, unknown to him, was about to come to an end.

I was paged to attend the scene of a burglary in what I would describe as a leafy suburb of North Down. A lady had locked her home and went to bed but during the early hours of the morning she was disturbed by someone entering her bedroom, via a side opening window. The burglar, on hearing her shout, made off from the scene and she phoned 999, and the police turned up promptly.

This bungalow was ideal, from a burglar's perspective, as the entire rear of the property was bordered by a high wooden fence. The police officers who attended the scene did an excellent job in preserving the potential evidence. The burglar had attempted to open the rear UPVC door, without success, but was able to gain entry through a rear bedroom window.

Having been disturbed by the homeowner, the burglar climbed out the open window and ran across a flower bed, climbed over the rear wooden fence, and made off. Police searched the surrounding area with negative results. Could the person responsible for this burglary be the one whom CID were looking for?

On examination of this scene, I recovered a partial footwear mark on the interior surface of the bedroom window sill. The direction of this impression proved that someone had stepped into the bedroom from the rear garden.
The flower bed only contained scuff marks, so I obtained soil samples. This potential evidence could be examined, later, by forensic scientists, against a suspect's footwear, should any be submitted.

Examination for fingerprint evidence proved negative. I also taped suitable surfaces where I thought fibres would be recovered, such as the area of fencing that the burglar had clambered over. It is all about connecting a suspect to the crime scene through trace contact or an item that has been abandoned at the scene.

I am not a forensic scientist, but the partial footwear mark was poor in its detail. The soil sample was questionable unless there was something unique in its composition and any fibres that one finds under the tape lifts are rebuttable in court unless they are unique.

This all-sounds doom, and gloom and it is, but the burglar had left something of interest behind. He dropped a small, black coloured, metal tool at the rear of the property when he was making good his escape. Would this mistake be crucial and would it give the investigating officers their first break?

Having completed my scene examination, I attended my favourite CID office and handed over my exhibits, apart from the small metal tool. At this stage you may be asking yourself the question, 'were the usual refreshments provided?' You should know better than to ask. The ladies provided tea and two buttered coconut finger rolls. What a team!

Now back to this tool. I needed to do some research into this metal bar before I handed it to CID as it held the potential for a much-needed breakthrough in the case. So what information could I obtain from this tool?
This small, insignificant looking tool was manufactured in a foundry located in the state of New York, USA, from where it was shipped around the world.

The manufacturers informed me that they exported it to a sole importer in the United Kingdom, based in Birmingham. I phoned this Birmingham company; the manager informed me that the sole retail purchaser of this tool in Northern Ireland was a well-known DIY store.

Armed with this information I met with the detectives and handed over my report in connection with the tool. As a result of this information the two detectives, in charge of the case, viewed many hours of CCTV footage from the DIY store and identified an individual buying several of these small metal tools. The suspect was arrested, and warrants were obtained to search properties that were connected to him.

In one such property police recovered a substantial amount of cash and, during interview, he could not provide a credible reason for having this money. This small, insignificant looking metal tool, which was abandoned at a crime scene, turned out to be incredibly significant, as it set the wheels in motion in bringing a criminal to justice.

Unfortunately, the jail sentence was too charitable; but I am not the person who makes those decisions.

Some months later a letter arrived on my desk, from police headquarters, acknowledging the role that I had played in helping bring this criminal to justice. I would have preferred it if the sender had come out from behind his desk and shook my hand; or he could have at least phoned me.

I have always believed and still believe that the personal touch works best, as it creates a sense of worth and respect. My parents taught me manners and to respect my elders and these lessons in life have served me well over the years.

I have examined burglary scenes where our senior citizens have been the victims of this callous crime and I have revisited some of these homes, several weeks after the event, to find that some of the victims had passed on and others were in nursing homes. This may have been due to natural causes, but I am sure that having one's home invaded left its mark.

I have recovered a whole spectrum of evidence at burglary scenes over the years; blood, saliva, head hair, fingerprints, footwear marks, cigarette butts, glass, casts of footwear marks, tools, and tool marks; the list goes on.

Various experts have examined the evidence I collected, and in some cases, this resulted in criminals being brought to justice. There were a few times where I managed to recover the full set of evidence types at one burglary scene. If only all burglars were this careless.

There have been some scenes, with regards to volume crime, which made me smile. I wish to point out that my personal joy in no way detracts from the seriousness of the crimes.

Police informed me that an elderly couple had returned from holiday to find that their home had been broken into and a substantial amount of jewellery, small electrical appliances, a compact music centre and music CDs had been stolen. I attended the scene, and the couple took me into each room and pointed out where their property had been.

Some of the jewellery was of great sentimental value and at this point the lady of the home had to be consoled by her husband.
The burglar had gained entry to their home by forcing open a rear ground floor kitchen window. This burglar was interested in anything that was small and thus easily carried; everything he collected he placed in a pillowcase belonging to the residents, and then he exited the same way.

There was a back door key on the kitchen work top, at the point of entry, yet the burglar climbed out through the point of entry rather than use the key. Sometimes the thought process of a burglar inwardly amused me. I have examined scenes where the burglar would make a cup of tea and wash the cup.

Now back to my examination of this scene. I had found only smears, up to this point in my examination, but there was one area still to be examined. The small music centre and numerous music CDs had been in the rear living room, but the area where it had been sitting also proved negative. I then noticed a single CD, on the mantelpiece to my right.

The gentleman told me that this CD had been on top of the music centre when they left for their holiday. The music on the CD was recorded by a well-known and much-admired Irish singer, from Donegal. This was the final piece of property that I examined. By the way I am also a fan of this artist.

The burglar was clearly not a fan of this singer's music; he had discarded it on the mantelpiece. I examined the CD and recovered fingerprints from its surface. I submitted this potential fingerprint evidence, along with elimination fingerprints of the elderly couple, for expert examination and several weeks later the results were in.

The fingerprints from the scene matched fingerprints held on record and the suspect was arrested and charged. Unfortunately, the property was not recovered.

So, a giant of the Irish music industry had indirectly helped us catch a thief, which still makes me smile with joy. I would love to tell him how he indirectly helped to solve this crime.

In today's climate of budget austerity, many cases like this would be recorded as a crime statistic and deemed not worthy of tasking police and in turn a CSI. How times have changed.

In this next case I was on call-out duty when police phoned me, at home, to attend a County Antrim police station, to examine a suspect who had been arrested for armed robbery of a well-known jewellery business in Belfast. Unknown to this individual, the jewellery business was protected by a product known as Smart Water.

Smart Water is a clear liquid, which contains a microscopic numerical code that is unique to each individual premises to which it is assigned. If someone breaks into a property where this deterrent is employed, the delivery system is triggered, and the culprit is sprayed with an extremely fine mist of clear liquid. The mist is so fine that the culprit or culprits do not realise that they have been covered in a unique marker.

On arrival at the custody suite, where this suspect was being held, I was met outside the interview room by a local detective; he briefed me on the incident and the circumstances leading to the arrest. The suspect had been arrested at his home a few hours after the crime. The police were hoping that he had not changed his clothes. If he was the culprit in this crime, and not too fussy about his appearance, he was about to get a shock, should my examination prove positive.

I entered the interview room, with eager anticipation, where I spoke with another detective. I introduced myself to the prisoner and placed a small black case on the table in front of him. He looked at the case and then in my direction but did not speak.

I informed him that I could connect him to the crime by merely looking at him. His reply was brash and offensive; he was noticeably confident as well as very rude. I told him to remain calm and all would be revealed soon, but I had to endure another round of nasty words in the meantime.
I opened the small black case and lifted out a square torch; the prisoner enquired as to its use. Funny how he was now interested in what I was about to do. The other detective had been waiting patiently by the light switch as we entered the room, after the initial briefing. I asked him to turn off the light. I waited for a moment so that our eyes were adjusted to the darkness and then I turned on the curious little torch.

The torch was fitted with an ultraviolet bulb and when I shone it at the prisoner it was clear to see that he had not changed his clothes. His clothes, footwear and the exposed areas of his body lit up like a yellow version of the Aurora Borealis! Smart Water fluoresces under ultraviolet light, so he was well and truly caught. Great result!

There was no staining to his face or head but there was a substantial amount on his neck and wrists. This told me that he had worn gloves and a head covering during the commission of the crime. So even if he had changed his clothes when he got home, he would still have been caught by this examination. I provided the suspect with a scene suit to change into; I took his clothing and footwear as evidence. I handed over the sealed evidence and advised the detectives to submit the clothing and footwear for forensic analysis for comparison with the Smart Water canister from the premises. No cursing now. The dazed look on the prisoner's face was worth being called out of bed for. The five hours overtime and mileage also helped.

This next case concerns the burglary of a house and garage while the owners were on holiday.

The burglar forced entry to the garage, removed a garden spade, and used it to lever open the patio doors at the rear of the property. Having gained entry and probably because he had not found anything of interest, he caused extensive damage throughout the interior of this property; however, he somehow managed to avoid leaving anything of an evidential nature.

I photographed the damage and took some paint, carpet, and glass samples, on the off chance that he would be caught in the commission of a crime later that night or the next day. One can always hope. I then examined the garage where I noticed a cigarette butt on the garage floor, which I photographed and recovered.

I submitted this cigarette butt for DNA analysis and the DNA recovered from it matched a DNA profile on the Northern Ireland DNA Database. Police arrested the suspect, interviewed him, and released him on his own bail awaiting trial.

Several months passed before I found myself waiting to give evidence in this case.

The defendant had maintained that he was innocent. His defence was that someone had stood on the cigarette butt and had carried it into the garage, on the sole of their shoe, where it fell off onto the garage floor. A fair defence, you would think.

It was clear that his counsel had never looked at the butt and had just assumed that it was flat. This was the next case to be heard. However, during the lunch recess, we were informed that the defendant was going to change his plea to guilty. Many cases have been sorted out during the lunch break. The cigarette butt in question showed no sign of having been stood on and so the matter was resolved before going to trial. I wonder if the defence team claimed their fee.

This next case was one that made me appreciate how fortune I was in being able to provide for my children. I was paged to attend the scene of a house burglary, on a large housing estate in Newtownabbey, Co Antrim. I knocked the front door of the property and when the door opened, I stood facing a young woman holding a baby in her arms. I introduced myself and on entering the house another child ran down the stairs, to my right; this little fellow introduced himself and asked me who I was. A cheeky chappie. I inwardly smiled.

We all entered the living room, and I stood in silence, for a moment, while I absorbed the scene of poverty laid out in front of me. Let me paint you a mental picture of this view. There were dead flies stuck to the windows, dirty dishes in the sink, the carpet was almost threadbare; you could carve your name in the dust and the seating was of landfill quality. There was a yellow-coloured baby bath on the living room floor doubling as a toilet. It was about a third full of urine and floaters. You have the image by now.

The young lady explained that, while she was out, someone had forced the back door open, took money from the living room and, tried to set the bed on fire in the upstairs front room.
I examined the alleged point of entry, which showed signs of old damage, and the area where the money had been also proved negative for anything of evidential value. Throughout this examination my brain was multi-tasking to try and find a way to help this young family, because they really needed support.

My next task was to examine the alleged arson scene, in the upstairs bedroom.

I asked everyone to remain downstairs, but the young boy wanted to go with me; there was a brief discussion and then my apprentice and I went off to examine the bedroom. His mother told me that he was almost six. To me he looked six going on sixty, but he seemed a lovable child. There was nothing in the house that led me to believe that a father figure lived there.

When we got to the bedroom, he told me that this was his room. I could see several areas of scorching on the bed sheet. I knelt beside the young chap and whispered to him. 'Did you set fire to the bed sheet?' He replied, 'Yes but don't tell mummy.'

We talked for a bit about the dangers of fire and then we struck a deal, sealed with a handshake. I promised him that I would not tell his mummy if he promised not to set the bed on fire again. Then he told me that he had tried to set fire to the bed because he was cold. What a sad situation.

I explained to the lady that police would be in touch and that I had found no evidence. As I was leaving the young boy pulled my jacket and gave me the thumbs up sign and I reciprocated. Before leaving the area, I contacted the police officer in charge of the case and explained that I had found no evidence; but I told him we needed to meet as there were more urgent matters to discuss.

The investigating officer took my recommendations on board and contacted the duty social worker, in my presence. Before finishing duty that day, and for my own peace of mind, I contacted social services; mercifully, they confirmed that they had been out to the house and the welfare of this family was now being taken care of. I often wonder how life turned out for this family.

I could have just left but in a lot of cases you need to take off the forensic hat and consider the welfare of those souls less fortunate than yourself. There but for the grace of God go I.

The following case is another one that also made me smile.

It had been one of those chocolate bars and fizzy drinks days, where the hours fly by and then it is time to go home. It had been an extremely busy shift, with no time to have a proper meal. I was looking forward to my pillow.

The pillow had cradled my head for around three hours when the home phone rang. I thought, 'Once more unto the breach, dear friends, once more' but hopefully, in this case, the task will not be difficult, and I will succeed in recovering evidence.

An officer in Belfast Regional Control (BRC) informed me that my presence was required at the scene of a burglary in North Belfast; the owners were not at home and could I contact the detective in charge, who was waiting at the scene.

A detective who attends a burglary scene in the early hours of the morning, would usually secure the scene and contact us later, when the morning shift starts, unless there was an urgent need for a SOCO to attend. I made the call.

My colleague was a seasoned detective; he told me he believed that there was an illegal firearm in the property. He said that 'Felix' had been tasked and would attend as soon as possible, as they were busy at another scene. 'Felix' is the mascot adopted by the Explosive Ordnance Disposal (EOD); 'Felix the cat with nine lives.'
Their role, at a scene like this, would be to x-ray the firearm, to make sure that it is safe; then they would hand me the x-

ray and I would submit it, along with the firearm, for forensic examination.

I drove to the office in Tennent Street, picked up the crime scene car and hurried over to the house. I spoke with the detective; he said he had no estimated time of arrival for the EOD team. We entered the house, where he pointed to the handgun.

The weapon was on a sideboard and there were several rounds of ammunition beside it. I stood in silence, looked at the weapon and ammunition and pointed to a photograph on the living room wall. It took a few seconds but then the penny dropped.

The photograph depicted a gentleman, splendidly attired in a cowboy outfit and holding the handgun in front of us, or at least a remarkably similar one. I told the detective to cancel the EOD. Thankfully, they were still unavailable.
We found information in the house explaining that the owner regularly competed in quick draw competitions. I made sure that the weapon was safe, and I checked the cartridges, which were all blank rounds.

For the uninitiated, a blank round if discharged, at point blank range, at someone, can cause severe injury or in some instances death. I left the weapon and blanks in the capable hands of the detective so that he could carry out the necessary enquiries. He needed to make sure that the resident was legally entitled to have this weapon and the blank rounds.

He apologised for getting me out of bed for nothing, but I told him that it was OK, as I would be claiming five hours overtime and mileage. We smiled knowingly at each other, and I left the scene.

I got to the office later that morning to find that the bush telegraph had already been distributed; funny, I thought, the article had no input from me. My handgun call-out had, to use current terminology, gone viral. There was a caricature on a Wild West style wanted poster, depicting the detective, which circulated for a while along with the alias of 'Quick Draw.' Humour at its best.

# Chapter 6

## Serious & Complex Offences

The following scenes, all of which I either examined or reviewed, fall within the category of serious and complex offences.

I was asleep, at home, when local police contacted me to attend the scene of a serious assault, at a dwelling located in a North Belfast housing estate. The location of this scene meant that police had to secure the dwelling and the surrounding area, for fear of a terrorist attack, prior to my attendance.

Scenes like this had the potential of becoming life-threatening in a matter of seconds. Naturally, should my colleagues come under attack, the scene would be abandoned immediately, as preservation of life is paramount. There have been several scenes, during my career, which needed to be vacated due to an imminent threat to life.

This was a complex scene, so I contacted a photographer and mapper to meet me in my office. The scene was still being secured, so we just had to wait, drink tea and swap war stories. Around an hour later a police patrol, in an armoured Land-rover, arrived to take us to the scene.

On arrival at the scene we were briefed, outside the front door of this terraced house, by one of the detectives in charge of this case. The other investigating officer was at a Belfast hospital, with the injured party, passing on as much information as he could get to police at the scene.

Here is what police knew at this stage in the investigation. The young couple that lived in the house were planning to have a night out, but then the lady of the house changed her mind, so the man decided to go out for a few refreshments by himself.

Some time passed and this lady decided to call in at a local club, which was on the estate. The club was run by local people for local people. It was the type of watering hole where a stranger would be spotted within seconds. It was in this club that the incident started. Her partner decided to call in at the club on his way home; when he got there, he noticed his girlfriend dancing with another male.

Once they were outside the club the red mist descended and, within seconds, an intense and abusive argument started.

Police received a complaint about a disturbance inside their home and on entering they could see that someone had been seriously assaulted; however, no one was at home.

The young woman had been placed in a taxi by her partner, who told the driver to take her to a hospital, as she was ill. He did not accompany her to the hospital.

On her arrival at the hospital, staff rushed her into the emergency department where, after a preliminary examination, medical staff realised that her internal injuries were life-threatening. Police, at this stage of the investigation, suspected that her partner was responsible for the assault, and he was subsequently arrested.

So why and how did this young woman sustain these horrific injuries? I am not going to describe her injuries to you; I am quite sure that once I have given you the details of what we found in the house, your imagination will be sufficient to paint you a picture of the horror and brutality that occurred there.

I arrived at the scene with my fellow experts and after we had suited up, I cleared a path to areas of forensic interest, of which there were many. Here is what I found during my examination of this scene, prior to recovering the potential evidence.

On the kitchen floor, beside the washing machine, I noticed clothing and trainers that were blood-stained. These items were recovered by the police, on my instructions. I walked up the stairs; there I noticed a broken hurling stick, on the dark brown landing carpet, outside the rear bedroom door, which was directly in front of me. The bathroom was to my right and the main bedroom was across the landing, to my left. On looking up, at the ceiling, I saw a piece of a hurling stick protruding from the trap door to the roof space.

A hurling stick, or hurley, for the uninitiated, is made of wood from the ash tree. This piece of sporting equipment is well known for its strength and reliability and so a considerable amount of force would be required to split it. Those who play the sport know the impact it makes when it collides with a surface.

On entering this rear bedroom I saw a single bed, immediately to my right, which had shoelaces tied to the corners of the headboard and footboard. These laces had clearly functioned as restraints; there were numerous spots of dried blood on the bedroom wall, directly above the bed.

It was clear to me that the young woman had been forcibly tied to the bed, against her will, and subjected to a sustained and savage beating with the hurling stick.

At this point in my examination of the scene I asked police to get me an update from the hospital as to her condition. A member of the trauma team informed the police that she had been sedated, so that medical staff could better assess her injuries; it seemed that she would remain sedated for the near future.

What possesses someone to carry out such a sustained and vicious attack? After I had examined, and recovered potential forensic evidence, from the landing, the trap door in the ceiling and rear bedroom, I moved on to the main bedroom.

As I stood on the landing, looking into this bedroom, I could see a large area of red and yellowish staining on the fitted sheet. The area of staining was slightly larger than a dinner plate; on closer inspection it was damp, as was the corresponding section of the mattress below the stain. There were also several large droplets of blood just beyond the main stain which were bright red and still damp. This staining was clearly a combination of blood and bodily fluids. The question was: what had taken place, on this bed, to cause such a stain?

Here is my interpretation of events, thus far.

This young woman had been subdued, tied to the bedframe in the rear bedroom, and then assaulted with a hurling stick. The assailant untied her from the shoelace restraints, carried her into the rear bedroom and put her on the bed. This was unlikely to have been a gentle arrangement.

I know what you are thinking: could the assailant have dragged her into the main bedroom? I thought of that, but I could not see any signs of drag marks on the pile of the landing carpet. You may also be wondering if this frenzied assault could have started in the main bedroom. The answer to your question lies with the condition of the blood staining.

The blood on the rear bedroom wall was dry, while the blood on the bed in the main bedroom was still damp and red.

My hypothesis of events held fast, despite my efforts to disprove it. The last room to receive my attention was the bathroom.

The bathroom was clean and tidy, with no visible signs of recent use; that is to say, everything was bone dry. I noticed a cheese knife in a container, along with toothbrushes, on the bathroom window sill.

I do not know about you, but I do not keep my cheese knife in the bathroom.

The cheese knife was like a garden weed trying to disguise itself for fear of being uprooted.

This cheese knife needed to be plucked from its location and recovered for forensic analysis.

It turned out to be an extremely important piece of forensic evidence and here is why.

Medical staff had placed the young woman into a state of sedation to assist the healing process. Several days had passed before she had recovered sufficiently that the investigating officers were able to speak with her. On the day of her assault, she had only been able to give extremely scant information to the police concerning what had happened, as she was drifting in and out of consciousness.

Now that she was on the slow road to recovery, the police hoped that she would be able to tell them about what had occurred.

Unfortunately, she could not remember the exact details of what had happened in the house; with one exception.

She remembered being on the bed, in the main bedroom, where her partner pulled down her jeans and underwear and started to insert what she thought was a cheese knife into her body.

It was then that she lost consciousness.

I am in no doubt that this young woman believed that she was about to die.

The suspect maintained that he had come home and found that she had been assaulted, so out of the kindness of his heart he ordered a taxi. Perhaps he had a phobia of ambulances, and in this case hospital as well.

No disrespect intended to those who have such fears; my wife tells me that I have a self-taught degree in sarcasm.

Several months had passed and everyone and everything was prepared and ready for trial. This trial took place in the High Court, Crumlin Road, Belfast.

I am sure that many of you have given evidence, over the decades, in the courtrooms located within the walls of this building.

This once impressive building is now a derelict shell, with vegetation as its only residents. What a shame. It could only happen here.

Many countries would have preserved such a property for generations to come.

It would have made an excellent attraction and investment.

Someone with vision could have used it to stage mock trials, or it could have been used as a movie set.

The witness box can be a lonely and isolated place, for some. Added to this, the imposing internal layout of the No.1 Court created an atmosphere where a shrinking violet's lifespan could be measured in moments; and this was before the case opened.

I have given evidence hundreds of times and in several courtrooms across Northern Ireland, during my career. Some of these trials had a jury present while others were Diplock trials; they were presided over by a judge sitting without a jury.

In this case the defendant had entered a plea of not guilty and decided on a trial by jury. Choosing those who would form the jury was a mini drama, where the defence and prosecuting counsels, including the judge, had an input in the process.
I knew the defence counsel well. We had crossed swords in the nicest conceivable way of course, many times before.

I cannot speak for others but my personal approach to giving evidence during a trial has its roots rigidly fixed in the art of drama. I had a role to play, and I would do it to the best of my ability. I had a few rules when I gave evidence and I adhered to them, always. This is my recipe.

Deliver the oath with confidence, tell the truth, stick to what you alone know, keep your answers short and precise, do not try and guess the next question and do not appear arrogant.

The jury had been sworn in, and they had listened to the opening speech, from the Crown Prosecutor, outlining the incident and other issues in connection with the case. Several witnesses had given evidence for the Crown and now it was my turn to enter the witness box. I had a routine, in such trials, which I repeated every time, during the short walk to the witness box.

I would always glance at the jury on my way to the witness box and maintain eye contact when addressing the jury with my answers. I would also make eye contact with the judge if a question came directly from the Bench.

The patina of this witness box was familiar to me and so I settled in and got ready to deliver my evidence, like so many good and true people have done before.

Please indulge me; I would like to take your thoughts away from this trial for a moment, to pay tribute to the Crown Prosecutor, who sadly is no longer with us.

He was a man who had great public spirit and his court presence instilled confidence in those witnesses who needed a little extra positive reinforcement, before encountering counsel for the defence.

Please accept my apology but I see no need to inform you of the precise details of the questioning that passed between the Crown and me. It is sufficient to put it this way. I just delivered my evidence, to the judge and jury, in respect of the questions put to me by senior counsel representing the Crown.

It was now the turn of defence counsel to ask me questions, but not until after lunch; 'all rise.' The court canteen was compact, in relation to the size of this court building and you could say it was cosy, given the number of people crammed into the space.
On the plus side, the snacks were tasty, staff were pleasant, and the banter was good.

On this occasion I was standing in the queue when counsel for the defence joined the queue behind me. We had a short, polite conversation. I asked him to go easy on me in the box and he just smiled, as did I. We knew each other as we mixed in similar circles, monthly.
Once lunch was over, followed by toileting I was ready to be cross-examined.

The court clerk called out my name and I walked towards the witness box. I went through my usual routine, and I was already under oath. Be seated.

I had answered several questions from defence counsel and the next exhibits, up for debate, were the pieces of hurling stick.

These exhibits were sealed with health hazard tape, visible on the exterior of the original packaging.

They had been visually examined by forensic scientists before being treated with chemicals which are considered hazardous to health.

You can imagine my surprise when defence counsel asked me to open the packaging in court, especially as there was a report and witness statement from the forensic scientist, in charge of this case, detailing what was found and the treatments used.

I looked at the judge, explained the potential risk, and said that the forensic scientist was present in court and would be better qualified to discuss these items, with respect to forensic issues. The judge was confident that I could undertake this task.

I informed the court that I did not have a protective mask or gloves in my possession.

It was then that I heard a familiar voice behind me, a voice that still resounds in my ears when I think about this case. It was the forensic scientist who had examined the pieces of hurling stick; she offered the court the use of a mask and gloves, which she produced from her handbag and the court accepted. Nice touch.

Perhaps she had been in the Girl Guides and was merely fulfilling one of the guiding principles of helping. I could only laugh, inwardly of course. Now I was attired with gloves and a mask, defence counsel asked me to open the exhibit bag that contained a piece of the hurling stick.

I informed the court that I needed a scalpel or a pair of scissors and, you guessed it, the same Good Samaritan came to the rescue. I wonder if there was a kitchen sink on offer. Let us get back to the trial.

Having opened this exhibit, the defence counsel asked me to measure this piece of the hurling stick. I needed a ruler.

I know what you are thinking; well, park that thought. What did I tell you about attempting to guess what will happen next?

There was no ruler in the handbag, surprise, but the court clerk saved the day. How fortunate.
If I had been on the jury, I would be wondering if this was a serious trial or a comedy of errors. This defence barrister was always theatrical in front of an audience, but he was also very precise.

I had just taken possession of the ruler, and I was about to measure the exhibit when the defence broke my gaze with an impertinent interjection. He asked me to address the jury, giving my answer using the metric scale; and if I did not know where to find it on the ruler, it was located opposite the imperial scale.

I thought 'how helpful' but never mind; now it was my turn to repay his kindness.
With the ruler still in my hand, I started to measure the exhibit, which was longer than the ruler.

I was always taught to measure twice and during my second measurement I broke silence to confirm if my answer was to be in metric.

By asking this question I had to start my measurements from the beginning, as I had lost my point of reference.

Defence counsel confirmed the metric scale and gestured, by flinging back the bottom of his cloak in the direction of the jury, to show that he was growing impatient.

I hovered above the exhibit again with the ruler and began my measurements once more. At this stage I thought defence counsel was about to treat the court to a solo performance of an Irish jig.

Before I could give my answer, defence counsel supplied the measurement, in metric, to the court, and asked me if I agreed with it.

The judge asked defence counsel where he had obtained this measurement. He replied that he had quoted from the forensic report; on hearing this response the judge put an end to his line of questioning.

Defence counsel turned towards the Bench and replied in the usual manner by saying, 'No more questions for this witness, My Lord.' The judge looked in my direction, thanked me for my evidence and informed me that I was free to go.

This trial lasted several days beyond my performance and after submissions the jury retired to consider the evidence.

The prosecution believed that they had a convincing case and that the jury would find the suspect guilty as charged. After some hours of deliberation, the jury came back into court, where they informed the judge that they could not reach a decision.

The judge asked them to take more time; they did, but upon their return the decision had not changed. The judge, on hearing this outcome, thanked the jury and put the wheels in motion for a re-trial.

This poor young woman had relived her horrendous ordeal and would have to repeat the process soon. A few weeks later I received good news that the defendant had changed his plea to one of guilty. This of course saved the public purse the expense of another trial and this largesse on the defendant's part was no doubt reflected in his prison sentence. At least he was off the streets.

In this next case I was deprived from receiving duty free goods and I will never look at a chicken dinner in the same light again. So how do these things relate to the following crime scene?

Belfast Regional Control contacted me as my presence was required at a West Belfast police station, in connection with an explosion.

Police had received a phone call from an anonymous male caller, who stated that he had heard an explosion; he had told the police the address where it had occurred.

You could not get better information than that; or was he telling lies? It would not be the first time that police were ambushed on their way to such a call.

Homework completed; we headed out of the station.

The location of this alleged incident meant that I had to be driven to the scene in the all too familiar armoured Land Rover, known as a Tangi.

Police were already at the scene with a cordon in place. As the Tangi approached the scene, I noticed a large crowd of well-wishers waiting for the arrival of myself and the army bomb disposal unit.

For any of you who are not familiar with the arrival of an ATO, ammunitions technical officer, well, it is extremely noisy.

Standing on the footpath, outside this semi-detached, cream-coloured house, we could hear the ATO sirens in the distance. It was hard to believe that an explosion had taken place in this property. There were no signs of physical damage on the outside of the building. The front door, roof and windows were intact.

I started to think could this be a hoax call; either that, or terrorists were observing and making a video of security forces responding to a major incident.

With all agencies in place a police officer rang the bell, and a woman opened the door. The police officer was invited in after he had given our reason for being there, and the ATO followed. It was only a matter of minutes before the police requested my presence.

On entering the house, the living room/dining room was only a few steps ahead, the kitchen was on my right and the back door led into a rear garden area. I could see that the rooms were very tidy, and I complimented the owner, who thanked me.

I was about to upset the friendly rapport that we had just established by lighting her blue touch paper with a few choice questions.

There was a large circular dining table with chairs, and it was positioned beside the dining room window. This window frame had a roller style blind attached, which in turn was festooned with white net curtains. I will explain more about this table and net curtains in a moment, but first I had to ask the owner when she last vacuumed the floor.

She looked at me and I could see that she was wondering, why is he asking me this? She knew why. As she was answering, I told one of the police officers to seize the vacuum cleaner. On hearing this, her true self exploded out of her mouth, and she needed to be restrained. The police were about to remove her when I told them to wait; I still had three more questions to ask her.

Now back to the table and curtains.

This wooden and inlaid Italian style table was on trend back in the day, as were net curtains, in a certain style of property. These items were not to my taste but each to their own. My next three questions to her were, could she account for the small burn mark on the table, the screwdriver that had a minute piece of metal welded to it and the extremely fine red misting on the surface of the net curtains?

Now the police had to hold her back. I told them to remove her from the house and to remember to seize the vacuum cleaner. I briefed the ATO, along with those police still inside the property, as to what I thought had occurred.

Here is what I think happened.

The burn mark on the table had been caused by the actions of someone sitting at this table with a screwdriver in hand, busy making some kind of homemade explosive device using copper pipe, with mercury fulminate as the explosive of choice.

This compound is a primary explosive and it is extremely sensitive to friction.

I can imagine this idiot crimping the copper tube at one end and thinking to himself that all was going well, so far; then, with screwdriver in hand, he started to ram home the mercury fulminate.

The force behind the screwdriver ignited the explosive, welding a minute piece of metal to the shaft of the screwdriver, and resulting in fine blood spatter across the net curtains. The curtains were ruined. However, the table and screwdriver were still usable. Not an entire loss then.

So, the question was: where did the person responsible for the explosion go?

I was convinced that the injuries sustained by this trainee bomber were substantial and he would have needed urgent medical treatment.

So, we set about searching the property. Having completed the forensic and fingerprint examinations of the scene, I joined the search. The ATO and police had already found items of interest that could be used in bomb making.

No, I had not forgotten about the owner of the property. I enquired, and all was calm once she had been escorted from the house. Local police were looking after her welfare. However, the tranquil scene going on at the front of the property was about to be shattered.

With all the potential evidence bagged and sealed there was only one item still to be searched, the wheelie bin at the rear of the property.

Mask, suit and gloves on, I cut open two large paper evidence bags and placed them on the ground beside the bin. I opened the lid and gently emptied the contents onto the paper.

I was not looking forward to this smelly task, but it had to be done. While I was busy searching through the detritus the ATO and my colleagues were talking while watching me conduct this fingertip search.

What I found in this bin ranked as one the absolute best and satisfying finds in my SOCO career.

I am going to keep you in suspense for a brief time, so please bear with me.

I looked up and asked a police officer if he would get the owner, as I needed to talk to her, with the proviso that when he returned, he needed to have his colleagues with him.

Wait for it!
I am sure that many of you have heard, as have I, the phrase 'as rare as hen's teeth.' In other words, non-existent.
Much to my amazement I found someone's right index finger, neatly wrapped up in chicken skin, secreted inside the chicken carcass, and hidden in the wheelie bin.
Well, I am no vet, but I am quite sure that a chicken does not have fingers. What do you think?
When I held up the finger and asked the homeowner for an explanation, shouting, spitting, and kicking commenced.

I deposited the finger inside a suitable glass vial, packaged it, attached the exhibit label, and handed it to a detective who had been at the scene from the time police entered the property.
I instructed him to take the finger directly to Fingerprint Branch. Later that day we had the identity of the culprit. But the story does not end at this point in the investigation.
Around six weeks later I took a phone call from police headquarters regarding this incident. I was asked to provide

a list of duty-free items of my choice, as I was going to be giving evidence at The Criminal Courts of Justice in Dublin. I do not drink or smoke, but I forwarded the list for the benefit of others.

Unfortunately, nobody benefited, because two weeks later I was informed that my presence was not needed. The bomber had been medically treated and arrested in Dublin, and for whatever reason my evidence was surplus to requirements. Who knows what occurred. I certainly do not want to know. I hope that you have been enriched by this account of 'the chicken who gave me the finger.' A book title? Perhaps not.

It was the week before Christmas when I was contacted by the police in North Down; they required my presence at a crime scene, where an alleged sexual assault had taken place. On arrival at the scene, which was no more than a large expanse of open ground, a detective briefed me, but he could not tell me much; there was scant information about what exactly had taken place or the precise location of the incident.

The weather was closing in and the police had carried out a preliminary search in case there was potential evidence that would need protection should the weather take a turn for the worse. There was a cordon in place, which I had them triple in size, while we stood by, waiting for more information to emerge from the injured party. It was not long before this information was received.

Having examined the scene, and with potential evidence obtained, I signed out of the scene log and met with the detective in charge, in her office. I handed her the exhibits, which she signed, and I returned to the SOCO office. At this time, the full story of what had occurred was still developing. The following day I phoned the detective, and she told me the story that had been told to her.

A seventeen-year-old teenager left her home in Scotland, boarded a ferry, and arrived in Belfast. Now when I use the words *left* and *home* what I really mean is *escaped* and *squat*. She described her life as a living hell; according to her both her parents were 'druggies and alcoholics.'

Having arrived in Belfast she decided to visit a well-known County Down town and, after walking around for a while, she entered a local pub.

While in this pub she met two males, who bought her drinks. She thought that she was safe in their company, but this was not the case. These so-called men took her to an area of waste ground and sexually assaulted her.

Cases like this make my blood boil, to tell the truth. It took some time, but the assailants were eventually arrested and dealt with for their crimes.

So, what became of this young woman who arrived in Belfast with only the clothes on her back? I was determined to find out. It was the day before Christmas Eve when I located her. Police had liaised with Social Services, who in turn had housed her in a safe place in Newtownabbey. The detective gave me the number of her case worker and I made the call. I needed to know if she was coping and if there was anything I could do to help in some way. Her case worker, as you appreciate, could not give me much information, but I was told that she was receiving trauma counselling. I wanted to get her something and her case worker suggested clothing; then she thought about it and changed the request to money.

I left the office, withdrew enough money from a cash MACHINE and about thirty minutes later I was parked outside the Social Services House in Newtownabbey, County Antrim. I phoned the case worker; she walked out to the

SOCO car, and I handed over a Christmas gift with my best wishes.

Several weeks had passed when I received an envelope in the internal mail. I opened it and, on reading it, I stood up and went into the SOCO store to wipe away the tears. It was an unsigned note to thank me for the gift, which she had used to buy clothes. The next line took the feet from under me in an instant. It read, 'I never knew that a person like you existed in this world.'

The cards that life had dealt her were not fair and I have often wondered, down the years, if her life eventually took a turn for the better. I will probably never know. Perhaps she will purchase my book, contact the publisher and we can talk. I can only hope.

Mr Strain was a shift worker who was employed at a County Antrim meat packing plant. He was twenty-eight and lived alone. He was last seen alighting from a local taxi on Sunday, 31 May 1998. When he did not turn up for work, his father went to his flat, and when he got no reply at the door, he forced an entry. As the door flew open, his father found himself facing a scene of complete horror.

The blood-stained body of his son lay on the sofa in front of him. He had clearly suffered a brutal and sustained attack, which he sadly did not survive. When a child dies the parent's loss is irreparable and everlasting; but to have a life taken away in such circumstances is beyond comprehension.

I am quite certain that someone knows who carried out this murder, and the circumstance that led to Mr Strain's death. The scene was examined, potential evidence was recovered, and suspects were interviewed; but nobody has ever been charged with this heinous offence.

I reviewed this as a cold case and submitted my report to the senior investigating officer when I was working in RMRU. The Police Service of Northern Ireland put out another appeal to the public for any information, in 2013, but nobody came forward. There was one aspect of this case that I found worth reinvestigating.

A CSI had recovered a wristwatch from the communal hallway near Mr Strain's flat. Mr Strain Snr. identified it as belonging to his son and the police returned it to him. One scene photograph shows the deceased wearing a wristwatch. Now of course, he may have had more than one wristwatch. This was a brutal murder, and not a burglary gone wrong.

Could it be the case that the wristwatch, recovered in this hallway, fell off the arm of an assailant while he or she was fleeing the scene? What was it about this watch that made his father believe that it had been owned by his son?

I met with the lead forensic scientist in this case and discussed DNA opportunities in respect of this watch, should it ever become an item of interest, and he was positive in his response. However, I will never know if this avenue of inquiry was entered into as my employment at RMRU ended.

When one is reviewing cold cases, one needs to look beyond the obvious; it is surprising how often it turns out to be the minutiae that can solve a crime.

I was sitting at my desk writing statements when the phone rang. My presence was needed at the scene of a serious sexual assault, in an area known locally as 'The Sandies,' near

Lisburn, County Antrim. Detectives were at this outdoor scene awaiting my arrival.

Due to the location and the traffic at that time of the day, I gave them an ETA of one hour. When I arrived at the scene the rain clouds were gathering, so time was of the essence.

Suitably attired and accompanied by a detective, who briefed me on the way, we approached the scene cordon. The detective remained outside the cordon while I signed the scene log and entered. For the uninitiated, the scene log is a hard-backed yellow book, which contains information on who entered the scene, their purpose for entering, their signatures, and the time they entered and left.

The person in charge of this book is called a log officer. Some scenes, due to their complexity, can take days to examine and so there will be more than one police officer in charge of the log.

Let me set the scene of this vicious assault.

A man dressed in army style clothing, black boots, a balaclava and brandishing a knife, with leaves tied about his head and neck as camouflage, pulled a child and her two friends into an area of undergrowth and sexually assaulted her in front of her terrified companions. He told the boys to cover their eyes with their t-shirts and then he hit them. He blindfolded the girl with a scarf, removed her shoes, trousers, and knickers and told her to lie on the ground, where he raped her.

The poor, traumatised little girl was crying; the offender told her to stop. He said if she did not, he would kill her and the two boys. When the assault ended the man said he was going but would return in ten minutes. Once he left, they went to the girl's home and the police were contacted.

I was informed that a suspect had been arrested and that other crime scene investigators were on the way to examine his car, house, and a locker. So, how was he arrested so quickly? He had been seen in the area several times by residents and one of them had noted his car registration. The police traced the car, and he was arrested.

So, what was I looking for to link this suspect to the scene of this assault? The undergrowth was comprised of tall, dense bushes and briars, with a narrow, well-trodden path made of sandy compacted soil, and patches of coarse grass. It was a perfect natural hiding place to lie in wait for someone to come along or drag someone into; in this case a young girl and two young boys. I arranged for the scene to be photographed and mapped prior to my examination.

I took samples of the diverse types of flora, along with soil samples. I searched the area for footwear impressions, bodily fluids, smoking materials, torn clothing, and fibres. I was looking for anything to link a suspect to this scene.

During my examination I found a small button, which I recovered as potential evidence. From its appearance it had not been in the undergrowth for a long time. Did this button belong to the suspect? The rain was imminent. I gathered the potential evidence, which was bagged and sealed, signed out of the log, went back to the scenes of crime car, and completed my scene notes.

While I was working at the attack site my colleagues were examining the suspect's car, home, and a locker of interest. Remember what I have already told you about cross-contamination, hence three separate CSIs. These three locations yielded potential evidence.

A search of the offender's locker at the Territorial Army Centre in Abbott's Cross, Newtownabbey, County Antrim, produced a camouflage jacket, black army boots and a black scarf. The scarf was later found to have attached to it several hairs which were forensically indistinguishable from the hair of the victim. A briefcase in the offender's bedroom contained girl's knickers and vests, tissues, used condoms, newspaper cuttings about young girls, and a video depicting children at a dancing class. The video camera was focused on the girls' genital area. More items of girls' clothing were found in the offender's car. A briefcase found in the car boot was filled with girl's underpants.

The suspect was presented with the evidence during several interviews. He did not admit to the crime, so the case went to trial. The only redeeming feature was that the children did not have to appear in court. Their statements were accepted by defence counsel. His father sat in the court every day of the jury trial, with his head cradled in his hands most of the time. I was in no doubt that this man was utterly ashamed to call the defendant his son. However, I gave him credit for attending court to listen to the evidence.

The barrister for the prosecution set the tone for this trial with his opening line. He pointed to the defendant, while looking at the jury, and uttered the words, 'That man stuck his penis in an eight-year-old girl's vagina.' Shock was visible on every juror's face. He informed the jurors that there would be more graphic details to come.

A consultant gynaecologist gave oral evidence to the judge and jury outlining the young girl's injuries. I can assure you that it was indeed graphic. Now it was time to introduce more evidence.

At this point in the trial the defence barrister needed to discuss a matter of law, with the jury not present. The judge excused the jury and listened to the defence barrister's submission in respect of the defendant's briefcase, containing girl's underwear and similar evidence.

The barrister suggested that if this type of evidence were introduced to the jury that it would be prejudicial to his client, as it would predispose them into thinking that his client was a paedophile. As this could affect the verdict, the judge accepted his submission and called the jury back. For me he was a paedophile and rapist.

The trial lasted five days and then it was time for the jury to retire and consider the evidence. At this stage in any trial, a Judge will address the members of the jury, outlining the evidence that has been placed before them, and remind them of their duties. However, during his summing up, the judge mentioned the briefcase containing girl's underwear. I looked at the detectives and they stared back at me. We could not believe what we had just heard.

The barrister for the defence sprang out of his chair, like a greyhound out of a trap, directed his outrage at the judge and called for a mistrial. The Judge, due to an error of his own making, declared a mistrial, thanked the jury and we all left the courtroom bewildered. Another trial was scheduled but before it took place the rapist pleaded guilty, and he was jailed for five years.

This five-year jail sentence was appealed to the Attorney General.

After due diligence it was concluded that this sentence was unduly lenient, and the tariff was increased to nine years. Do you think that nine years served as a deterrent? I do not.

# Chapter 7

# A Reasonable Request

David Hamilton lived in a first floor flat at 26H Gleneagles
Gardens, Belfast.

No motive was ever established for this murder but having
interpreted the crime scene I am offering up this scenario as
a possibility of what took place, on a small communal
landing, outside 26H Gleneagles Gardens, Belfast, on 29<sup>th</sup>
November 2004.

This communal area was wet and David's lifeless body,
which was inside his flat on arrival of police, was also wet.
I believe that David was assaulted in this communal area and
water was used to wash away the evidence. So here is my
theory of what had taken place.

If my next-door neighbour is having a party and/or playing
loud music, I would ask him, in person, if he could keep the
noise down. I do not think that such a request is

unreasonable, especially if I am starting work early in the morning.

This assumption is formed because I know that my next-door neighbour is a responsible person. However, as you know, not every neighbour is reasonable.
Some people have aggressive natures, per se.

David was to start work early that morning. So, was his neighbour noisy? Did he knock his neighbour's door, with a reasonable request to keep the noise down?
If this was the case such a request cost him his life.

David, at the time of his death, was employed, as a porter, in a nearby hospital, about a twenty-minute walk from his first floor flat. This is the same hospital where I had examined the scene of that accidental death on Christmas Eve, 1997.
The people who confronted David, on that November day in 2004, were not believers in the concept, 'Thou shalt love thy neighbour as thyself.'

This gentleman was cornered in a small communal landing, with no way out, trapped like a fox facing a pack of rabid hounds bent on taking life.

When I attended such scenes, I was not concerned with why someone had taken a life, I was there for the deceased.

My role was to do everything, within my power, to recover anything, of an evidential nature, which could be used, later, to convict someone of the offence.

In this case, the murder of David Hamilton.

On 29<sup>th</sup> November 2004, I was a CSI working out of Strandtown Police Station, Belfast, when I received a telephone call, from Belfast Regional Control, to attend the scene of a suspicious death.

Police had been tasked to a flat in Gleneagles Gardens, Belfast, where they found the dead body of a male inside this flat.

Having obtained a preliminary briefing it was clear to me that this was not a scene where everything was contained within a specific area, i.e. a single flat.

This scene needed to be assessed and managed, with a forensic strategy, put in place, to rule out cross contamination.

Let me provide you with a simple example of cross contamination, in relation to the recovery of potential evidence.

You have been tasked to a major crime scene inside a house and having just completed your examination you receive a request to examine a car, believed to relate to this incident. If you examine this car, having examined the house, this would be considered as a clear case of cross contamination.

I can hear you thinking, 'surely by wearing a new crime scene outfit, at the car, cross contamination would be ruled out?' You would be wrong in that assumption.

Let me fast forward to the trial where the defence counsel asks the question 'is it possible that some of the fibres and head hair, which you recovered in the house, could have been transferred to the car?' The answer to that is 'yes, it is possible.'

You could argue that by wearing a clean crime scene outfit cross contamination would be ruled out but by doing so you are leaving yourself open to further examination by the defence.
It is all about reasonable doubt and in this example the seed of reasonable doubt would be well and truly planted in the mind of the judge and jury.

Therefore, what was considered as being exceptional evidence is now tainted due to your actions.

What should have happened, in this example, is that another CSI, not connected with this case, examines the car thereby ruling out cross contamination.
Now back to the scene at Gleneagles Gardens.

Contamination of a crime scene is another matter that needs to be addressed, i.e. details of who had entered the crime scene, prior to my arrival, and what actions were taken.
Was entry forced to the flat? Who entered the flat? Were any items touched or moved to reach the body? Was the body moved?
All this information is vital and should be obtained from the first responders. I need to be in possession of this information before I enter the scene.

It may also be necessary to obtain DNA samples, fingerprints, and footwear impressions from all first responders for comparison and elimination purposes against the potential evidence recovered from the scene. A scene, such as this one, will always be contaminated as preservation of life is paramount.

I have attended major crime scenes where I recovered cigarette butts, within the police cordon, to find out later that they had been discarded by police officers guarding the scenes. Errors like this are due to a lack of thought and are easily corrected by a few choice words.

On my arrival at Gleneagles Gardens, I assessed the position of the police cordon.
The cordon needed to be extended to keep residents back and to take in a large, grassed area surrounding the property. Having been satisfied with the new position of the cordon I spoke with the police officer in charge of the scene log.

This officer had noted details of everyone who had entered and exited the scene, prior to my arrival.
At this stage life had been pronounced extinct and the police officer in charge of the scene log pointed out the common approach path before I got the chance to ask him. The log was in safe hands.

A common approach path is the route that everyone takes on entering and exiting a crime scene and, in this case, it was a paved area.

Let me expand on the term 'common approach path.'

I am sure that you have watched numerous crime dramas on television, where you see those who play the roles of investigators and CSIs arrive at the police cordon.

In some cases, before entering the scene, they use the term 'common approach path' or something similar and on they go chatting away as the drama unfolds for the viewer.

The adjective common is used in the sense that many people have used this approach path to enter and exit the scene.

In my mind that is where the use of the word common ends.

This approach path is anything but common, from a crime scene examination perspective, as the person or persons who committed the crime may have used it to enter and exit the scene.

I wonder how many approach paths did not receive the necessary due care and attention that they clearly warranted.

A police officer in charge of the scene log has a vital role to fulfil, as the written information contained within its pages must be accurate. In this case there were several scene log officers, due to the length of time it took to complete the scene examination. A crime scene log, once completed, is an important historical document containing a chronological list of events that took place during a crime scene examination.

I was about to make a request for the investigating officer to attend when he arrived at the scene along with the senior investigating officer.

It had been a while since the SIO, and I were together at a major crime scene. It was a nice touch when he looked at me and said, 'it's good to see you here.'
We had a brief but detailed conversation about the incident, and I continued with my preparation, prior to entering the scene.

There were four areas to be forensically examined at this incident; David's flat, the flat next door, the communal area, and the ground outside the property, which was within the police cordon. There were also suspects in this case.

This scene required multi agency teamwork and the calibre of people who arrived at the police cordon, to take on this task, were second to none. I can make this statement as I had worked with them before, at major crime scenes, over a number of years.

Consider, for a moment, any profession from the following perspective.

There are those who are exceptional at what they do, some are acceptable, while others manage to muddle through.

By this time, in my career, I had examined numerous scenes which resulted in a person's life having been cut short, due to the savagery of others. 'Did I ever get used to looking upon the results of such savagery?' Well, the answer to that, from my point of view, is 'Never.'

Such scenes can eventually be detrimental to one's psychological wellbeing, due to their traumatic nature and cumulative effect.

However, you are not necessarily aware of such pressure until a tipping point appears, from left field, and changes your character into something that no one recognises, including yourself.

I was aware that David's body was in the living room but until I could see him my mind could only present me with images based on information from the first responders.

Even though this gentleman was deceased I still liked to use his name rather than terms such as the deceased, the body, or the remains. For me, this approach worked best, as it was more reverent and less clinical.

Please follow me, as I allow you to invade my thoughts and space, during my examination of this scene.
With the small communal hallway having been examined I am ready to enter the main scene.

I am now, suitably attired and standing outside the open front door of David's flat.
Looking down the narrow hall I can see that the living room door, which opens to the right, is ajar, affording me a view into an area of the living room.
I can see that there has been substantial damage to property, in this area of the living room, but, from my position, I have no view of David's body.

My priority is to clear a path, to recover David's body, as soon as possible.
However, based on what I can see, thus far, it will be tomorrow until I am able to have that duty performed.

Everything needs to be photographed and mapped prior to any examination.

So, the procedure is photograph, map, examine and then recover anything that is of an evidential nature.

Photographs and a detailed map of a scene, accompanied by my contemporaneous notes assist not only me but many others during and after the scene has been examined and closed.

Those with a personal stake in this information are the investigation team, the pathologist, the coroner and, in this case, the judge and jury.

The first area to be examined is the front door and frame for the presence of blood, fibres, finger/palm prints, footwear marks and any sign of damage.

This entry/exit point has been used many times over the years and in this case by the person or persons responsible for this crime.

Unfortunately, this area of the scene proved negative for anything of an evidential nature.

It is now time to remove my outer pair of Nitrile gloves, put on a clean pair, and step into the hallway, but it is not as simple as that.

Wearing disposable overshoes does not give me cart blanch to step onto the entrance hall floor and walk into the living room, to where David's body is.

'Why not?' I hear you ask, after all the first responders and others have already walked in and they had no protective clothing on.

In such a circumstance the preservation of life, as previously mentioned, comes first.

This entrance hall floor, for me, is an interior common approach path, which, despite being used by all, still warrants a fingertip examination of its surface.

To traverse this surface, I employed metal stepping plates. These square stepping plates are made of heavy gauge polished metal, with sufficient surface area for stepping and/or kneeling on. The four corners are about 75mm deep and function like a trivet when placed on a surface.

I can read your thoughts. 'Why not just place the stepping plates along the entrance hall floor and on into where David's body is located?' This method would get you into the living room in seconds.

That is true, it would be the quickest way into the living room, but by adopting this approach you run the risk of missing potential evidence, e.g. a spot of blood now covered with a hastily placed stepping plate.

It is vital that any area, where you need to place a stepping plate, is meticulously searched first, prior to covering it with the steeping plate.

Now you realise why it will take me a long time to reach David's body.

One can predict how long it will take to examine a crime scene once you possess the relevant information.

I informed the SIO that it would take me four to five working days to complete my part of the scene examination and that David's body could be removed by day two.

It is important to keep the investigators' informed, daily, with regards to progress and what has been recovered.

Having been at the scene for several hours I decided to have a short break.

Once outside David's flat I removed my protective clothing, placed them is a disposable bag, and signed out of the scene log.

It is essential, at this type of crime scene, to have a break at a time that suits you.
I know this area of Belfast and there is a small retail park, around five minutes' drive from the scene. I had lunch at this watering hole each day. I could have brought a packed lunch from day two onwards and dined outside the cordon.
However, I always maintained that it was important to have lunch away from such an intense scene.

This approach allowed me to maintain a physical barrier between the scene and myself. Looking in the direction of tragedy, while eating, is not good for the digestive system. If there is a colleague to go with you even better, as you can talk about everyday events together. However, no matter how hard you try, some thoughts of the scene will always seep through.
Lunch over it is now time to re-enter the scene. Attired in a new crime scene outfit I sign into the scene log and continue my examination of the entrance hall.

I am around halfway along the hall at this point in my examination. My goal was to finish the hall and get an area of the living room examined before stopping operations for the day.

Standing on a stepping plate, at the living room door, I looked into the room where I could see David's partially clothed body, on the floor, immediately to my left.
David's head and torso bore visible signs of trauma.
The contents of the living room had been smashed, and it was possible that some of the contents may have been used as weapons.

David had been bludgeoned to death during a prolonged savage and frenzied attack.
I closed my eyes and had a quiet moment of prayer and contemplation.
I can visualise David's lifeless body as I type.
My estimation was correct; reference the time it would take me to examine this crime scene.
The entire surface of the living room floor was covered with several types of broken glass. It was like a carpet of glass laid out in front of me.

The main contributor to the glass carpet was a smashed smoked glass pane that had been part of a coffee table. There was a red brick faced corner unit, directly in front of me, and the wooden top, for the unit, had been removed. This unit was where the television had stood and a recess, built into the unit, had housed a digital TV box. The TV was damaged, and the digital TV box had been ripped from its wiring.

My rage was palpable, as my mind began working through a strategy for examining what I saw in front of me. 'Why would anyone want to murder a hard-working hospital porter, whose role in life was to help others and earn a wage to support his family?'

There was a considerable amount of material to examine, before I could reach the location where David's body was lying, so a decision was made to finish for the day. I removed my scene clothing, placed them in a disposable bag and signed out of the scene log, as did my colleagues, who had been examining the flat next to David's. We had a short debrief, outside the police cordon, and left the scene.

The crime scene integrity was left in the capable hands of local police, who protected it overnight.

Suitably clothed I signed into the log the following morning and walked up the stairs to the front door of 26 H.

Everything was as I had left it the previous evening.

I walked on the stepping plates, that I had left on the entrance hall floor and halted on the last one to, once again, survey the carnage that I was about to examine.

It was a matter of repeating the process, of using the stepping plates, to reach David's body.

There were hundreds of glass shards, which were not suitable for fingerprint examination, due to having an insufficient surface area.

However, I visually checked each shard for the presence of blood.

My examination, of this area of the living room, took several hours and I was now within touching distance of David's body.

This was a suitable time to take a break, to recharge the batteries. I went through the usual routine and then drove to the same watering hole for refreshments.

Refreshments usually consisted of a sandwich, a chocolate bar and a small cup of tea or coffee.

Now back to the scene, to concentrate on the task at hand.

I walked along the well-trodden path, of stepping plates, to where David's body was lying. It was now time to examine this area of the scene, so that I could release David's body for onward transportation to the mortuary.

On closer inspection, of David's torso, I noticed an incised mark, which was familiar to me. I paused for a moment, deep in thought, trying to recall where I had seen this hexagonal shape before. I grabbed the sealed evidence bag that contained the digital TV box and looked at the rear of this item.

The ariel socket, which protruded beyond the rear perimeter of the box, had a hexagonal shaped tip and the outline of this stainless-steel tip matched the mark on David's torso. I concluded that this digital box had been used, as a weapon, during the murder of David Hamilton.

Other items that had been used, as weapons, in this sustained attack were a brick, a heavy smoked glass tabletop, several glass items from the mantlepiece and the wooden top from the corner unit.

It was now time for David and me to part company.

With assistance, I placed his body in a CSI body bag, attached the seal and my exhibit label and watched, in silence with head bowed, as he left his home for the last time. It was a solemn moment.

It was evident that David had been extremely house proud, as the interior of his home was immaculate and in stark contrast to the living room in which I was standing.
This had been another long day and so it was time to go through the usual routine and head home.

Standing in the shower, with the water beating down on my head, my mind was consumed with the need to link any suspects to this scene, through forensic and or fingerprint evidence.
I then heard a knock on the bathroom door and the voice of my daughter asking me if I was OK.
I had lost track of time, and I still needed to apply soap to skin and shampoo to head.

Walking down the stairs I was admonished by my other daughter, in a friendly tone, for taking too long in the shower. 'Touché.' I would usually complain about their shower time. The following days were consumed with the recovery of more forensic samples, from the living room, and the examination of numerous items for the presence of latent fingerprints. My examination of this scene was coming to a close.

On entering the living room there was a window to my left, with a bulky storage heater mounted on the wall below the sill. The carpet in this area was also covered in numerous pieces of broken class.
The confetti of glass, in this area, contained several pieces of glass that had a large enough surface area to warrant an examination for latent fingerprints.

So far, I had spent many hours using various fingerprint powders, on numerous suitable surfaces, in the living room, hoping to develop latent fingerprints/palm prints, with no success.

The marks that I had developed, of which there were many, turned out to be smears and smudges that contained virtually no ridge detail and therefore of no evidential value.

My frustration by now, in not finding sufficient ridge detail, for examination by a fingerprint expert, had almost reached its pinnacle.

If you can imagine holding the business end of a pin against the surface of a helium filled balloon and applying pressure, but not sufficient to burst the balloon, that would be a good analogy of my level of frustration.

This was a suitable time to step away, from this area of the living room, park my frustration and focus.

To achieve this, I read my notes, while remaining in the living room.

I was now ready to employ my working tools, for the last time, in the hope of an evidential reward.

Before continuing my examination, I closed my eyes, for a moment, and thought of David.

With only a few small pieces of glass remaining, to be examined, my hope for finding, potential fingerprint evidence was fading.

I had, by now, recovered many items from this scene, which I bagged and sealed for future submission to, Forensic Science Northern Ireland, where they would be examined by various forensic scientists, for potential evidence.

Now back to the few remaining pieces of glass, on the living room carpet, near the storage heater.

I lifted a piece of glass, about 20mm x 20mm, and applied black fingerprint powder to the surface, still in the hope of developing a latent print. One should never lose hope.

A latent print is not visible to the human eye but once the item is treated, in this case by applying black powder, ridges with appear, if present.

There are numerous powders available, for use by a CSI, and information about them is available, on the Internet, should you require it.

For the first time a latent mark appeared on the surface of this small piece of glass.

You have heard of the well-known phrase, a eureka moment, well I called this my 'yes' moment.

I shouted out the word yes and a colleague, from outside the property, asked if I was OK.

I was better than OK. I had developed a latent mark, with enough visible ridge detail to make the mark viable for examination by a fingerprint expert.

However, this mark had yet to be examined so, metaphorically speaking, I burst the helium filled balloon and brought my thoughts under control. I hoped that this mark was from a culprit and not David.

This small piece of glass would be a challenge to package, to protect the fragile ridges on its surface.

As part of my equipment I had a small flat pack style cardboard box, used for packaging a mobile phone.

I assembled my resources i.e. cardboard box, broad high tack tape, 2 x small acetate sheets and a permanent marker.

I was about to construct something that the late 'Heath Robinson' would have applauded. I took a small acetate sheet, stuck a loop of high tack tape to its surface and holding the glass fragment, along the outer edge, I pressed it onto the high tack tape, which anchored it in place, with the visible ridges facing up.

So far, so good, for this fragile cargo.

I penned my identification mark to the acetate, took the other acetate sheet and formed it into a protective canopy over the surface of the glass, which contained the ridge detail, and taped the edges, of this sheet, to the first sheet. The shape reminded me of a World War II air raid shelter.

It was not pretty to look at, but it was extremely functional.

I then placed the structure inside the cardboard box, ready for transportation.

I walked to the front door of David's home, handed my precious cargo to a colleague, with the strict instructions to hold it the way in which I had handed it over and to take it immediately to Fingerprint Branch.

I had entered 26H Gleneagles Gardens, Belfast, on Monday 29th November 2004 and left on Friday 3rd December 2004. The ridge detail, on this small piece of glass, was a match for a Mark Frederick Kincaid, who was arrested and subsequently charged with the murder of David Hamilton. I would like to think that David's spirit, in some way, guided my hand.

My colleague recovered evidence from the flat next door which resulted in the arrest of two evil individuals who were also charged with the murder of David Hamilton.

The CSI who examined the flat next door was the former St John's ambulance first aider who helped at the aftermath of the Shankill Road bomb scene, 23 October 1993.

William George Anderson, Gareth Colin Anderson and Mark Frederick Kincaid were found guilty of this brutal murder.

All three of the defendants pleaded not guilty and denied being in David Hamilton's flat. However, the jury found them guilty having heard the forensic and fingerprint evidence, presented at trial in 2007, which linked the accused to the murder scene.

The judge, Hart J, considered everything that had been said on behalf of each of the accused and informed the defendants that they would each serve the minimum term of 16 years imprisonment before they could be considered for release.

In 2009, the legal team for the prisoners, Mark Kincaid, and Gareth Anderson, lodged an appeal, on their behalf, against sentence.

The appeal judges reviewed the summing up of judge Hart J, the jury findings, and the evidence against the appellants.

The three appeal judges were satisfied that there had been sufficient evidence put before the jury and that it had not been shown that the conviction was in any way unsafe.

David was bludgeoned to death while all three of these murderers are now walking the streets. I wonder if they have ever thought about what they did back in November 2004.

# Chapter 8

## Stress Relief

I was sitting at my desk in the SOCO office, at Tennent Street RUC Station, finishing paperwork, when there were several explosions. These explosions sounded as if they were at the rear carpark, inside the station complex.

The phone rang and the duty officer told me that explosive devices had been thrown over the rear gate, landing in the carpark where we parked our private cars.

Police officers had cordoned off the area and the bomb disposal unit were on their way, to make the scene safe. It was possible that not all the devices had detonated.

Another phone rang and it was the captain in charge of the EOD unit; he asked if he could bring his entire team to the scene. We knew each other from past incidents but, as yet, I had not had the pleasure of meeting some of his colleagues.

The captain and his men arrived, and I took orders for a brew, while they walked off to deal with the devices. Just as he was leaving, the captain asked me if he could make a phone call, on his return, and he said that he would bag all the evidence for me. I of course said yes if it was not Australia.

While waiting for their return the mischievous side of me took over. I am sure that many of you had a cap gun during your formative years; well, I had something better and louder in my desk drawer.

I loaded this exceedingly small, spring-loaded, percussion cap striker, held it in place so that it would not go off in my hand and carefully put it below the handset of the phone, near where the tea tray was located. The device was now armed.

I had just finished pouring the teas when the band of innocents returned from the scene. Chocolate biscuits were also on offer. Nothing but the best for my army chums.

Having handed out the teas, with my poker face on, I sat back waiting for the show. Well, I was not disappointed and, as it turned out, neither were they.

The captain asked again to use the phone, so I pointed at one and he lifted the handset, which triggered the little device I had planted.

Some tea went into the air, while some was sprayed out of mouths. It was like the fountain display outside the Bellagio Hotel, Las Vegas. Then the laughter started, and they all agreed that the entertainment was excellent and in good spirit.

Before they left, the captain told me that he would repay the compliment at some future meeting, and he was as good as his word. However, that is a story for another time.

The senior man in our office appointed a member of our unit to make sure that the interior of each SOCO car was kept clean. The responsibility for stocking each car with scene equipment was the responsibility of the person who had used it last.

There was no point in assigning a specific car to each individual team because, at times, we used whatever car was available, due to the continuous and heavy workload.

Keeping all four cars clean, once a week, was a task undertaken when there was time to do it. I appreciated the effort put in to maintain each car. However, there were those who saw an opportunity to make mischief.

No, it was not me on this occasion.

The colleague who got the cleaning job was well qualified, as he put time into being tidy. Some believed that he was obsessive in the cleanliness department. Perhaps he had OCD. What I was sure of was that he had extreme patience.

When a car had been cleaned somebody would soon reverse the process by eating flaky food inside it and then depositing the crumbs everywhere. This prank, which continued for several weeks, was carried out to try and raise the blood pressure of the cleaner.

I must applaud the car cleaner because he never got annoyed, or at least if he did, he kept it to himself. The lengths that some people go to relieve work stress have no boundaries. The messy eater soon stopped having failed miserably to annoy our cleaner. I am sure some of you did worse.

The next prank took place while I was sitting at my desk.

I was about to eat my sandwiches when the office door opened. Three detectives, from another station, walked over to me and one of them sat down and asked me if I was free to attend a scene with them.

I told him that I was about to eat, but once I had finished, I would be free. The scene in question was one that needed an EOD unit to attend, to make it safe prior to my attendance. I lifted the phone and called the bomb disposal unit, and an ETA of thirty minutes was given, as they had just finished at another scene.

While I was on the phone one of the detectives was munching through my lunch. He was about to put mustard in my remaining sandwich when I multitasked. With my free hand I reached forward and grabbed the tube of mustard that was in his hand and squeezed it. This had the desired result; the mustard squirted onto his tie and shirt. Despite his efforts to clean the mess it still left two large, yellow-coloured stains.

A mustard stain is extremely hard to remove from material and his tie and shirt looked more expensive than my sandwich.

As it was going to take some time for the EOD to do their work, the detectives went to the canteen to get tea. As they were leaving, one of the detectives asked me if he could leave his overcoat; I said yes, and he hung it on the rear of the door.

Several minutes later, the office door flew open and out of the corner of my eye I saw a white liquid heading in my direction. I was sharp enough to lean back and let the liquid hit my desk and the floor. The Pranksters, for whatever reason, had hatched a plan, over tea, to launch milk at me.

No damage was done; after all it was only a spillage that could be cleaned. So, what could I use to clean up the mess? The cleaning cloth was hanging on the back of the office door. It was nice of the detective to leave his overcoat/cleaning cloth at my disposal.

It was a quality three-quarter length, hounds-tooth style woollen coat. I employed the exterior of his coat to mop up most of the mess, and the interior too. The interior was not as good a mop as it was made of polyester and did not soak up the milk compared to the exterior. Still, I thought, a job well done. I am sure you agree.

I had just put the coat back on the door when the detective returned for it and put it on. From his expression I noticed that he was not aware of what had taken place.

My pager went off and my presence was needed at the scene. I arrived at the RUC station that covered the area, so that I could be driven to the scene in an armoured Land Rover. Prior to leaving for the scene, I was met by the meal stealer, who informed me that his colleague had to leave to change his clothes, as he was wet through to his underpants, and that the car would need to be cleaned.

I told him that he had paid the price for playing against a stronger opponent.

This group of three detectives retired around the same time but sadly two of them are no longer with us, due to instant ill health. They did not get long to enjoy their retirement.

I had a lot of respect for these men, who were excellent at what they did. If I had needed to have a personal issue investigated, they would be my choice. I attended the funerals of Philip and Ricky. God rest their souls.

It was around seven in the morning when I returned to the station to complete paperwork, having been called out to a scene. When I got to the office, Jim, the oldest SOCO in the village, was at his desk, drinking tea and eating toast, as he too had been called out.

It took me about one hour to complete the paperwork and restock the scene car. During this time, the early crew had arrived to face the day. I walked into the rear room, put the kettle on and went to get my last two slices of bread to toast them; they were not there. I had to count to ten before asking who had taken my bread.

There was an instant confession from my colleague; he had been called out before me and, when he arrived back, he made tea and toast. I told him not to worry, but he handed me a £10 note and insisted that I take it and buy myself breakfast.

I went to the canteen and bought tea, toast and scones for myself, my colleagues and two CID officers who were also in our office. I placed the tray on my desk, told everyone that he had treated us to breakfast and handed back the small change. This was followed by a round of thanks from everyone.

Looking over the top rim of his glasses and with a wry grin he thanked me for bringing back some change. He informed me that he would not be caught like that again. I told him that it was a pleasure, while at the same time thinking about what form his revenge would take.

He was one of the founding fathers of SOCO but, sadly, he is no longer with us. I enjoyed his company, stories, and the dry wit of this former pupil of Portora Royal School.

I arrived in work, an hour early, as I needed time to write an urgent statement of evidence in connection with an incident that I had examined earlier in the week.

Most of my colleagues from the early turn were in the office, winding down before home time. On sitting down, I noticed a camel-coloured overcoat inside a plastic cover, the type that you get if you have taken an item to have it dry-cleaned. This garment was hanging on the wall at the back of Jim's desk.

I had never seen him wear this coat during the years I had known him, so I made a complimentary comment about it, but there was no reply. However, another colleague told me that it had been under his Irish Wolfhound for years, as part of its bedding.

On closer inspection of this coat I noticed that both man and man's best friend had made good use of it. Would I have brought it into the office to wear it once more? Well, if I did not have another coat the answer would be yes, but only when it was dark outside.

There were three of us on to cover the late turn that night and Jim was on a twelve-hour shift, finishing at seven, but he was available to return to duty if needed. His overcoat remained in the office when he headed home.

The shift was unusually uneventful and, having phoned Belfast Regional Control to pass on the callout rota, we headed for the door. It was then that my fellow SOCO had an idea. I must own up now because I was his accomplice.

One of our team did a lot of shooting and he had several large plastic decoy woodpigeons on his desk. Can you guess where this is going, or is it too early for you to work it out?

The decoys were strategically placed; two coming out of a Venetian style blind, one on a desk and two stuffed into the neck area of the camel-coloured overcoat. Like all good window dressers, we stood back to assess our work. Everything looked good; but it lacked something.

My colleague noticed a bottle of correction fluid beside the woodpigeon that was on the desk. You can now see where this was going. The fluid, being a decent match for bird pooh, was used to finish our installation.

We stood back, once more, to appreciate our efforts. It was a work of art that would not be out of place as part of the Turner Prize Exhibition; it was certainly at the same level of taste. Time to hit the road home.

I arrived in the office at seven along with the team covering the early turn. Our installation was still in place, for which we received a round of acclamation. Jim was the last to arrive and he remained silent as he walked to his desk. I cannot remember who it was, but someone remarked that the woodpigeons had made a mess and accused me of leaving an office window open.

A loud cheer went up, just as a few detectives entered the office. The detectives agreed that the artwork was outstanding. Still silence from our friend.

Back to work. Having removed the decoys, we all headed out to examine crime scenes, leaving Jim to run the office in our absence.

The shift was ending when a detective came into the office, with Jim behind him, sporting a devious grin. Payback time, I thought. As nobody had owned up to the prank we were cautioned for malicious damage of the overcoat, oh sorry, the Irish Wolfhound's bedding.

It was a lame retort at revenge, but we had to give him a certain amount of kudos for trying. The malicious damage caution went down in flames of laughter.

Before leaving to go our separate ways, I bought Jim a peace offering from the canteen and we smiled at each other. This was an office in which many would not have fitted in and one that produced strong-willed characters, both male and female. I was proud to have been part of this unit with all its idiosyncrasies. The overcoat was never worn in the work environment, so I am guessing that the Irish Wolfhound was pleased to receive its favourite blanket back.

I will end this chapter with a short story involving myself and my colleague Jim.

I had been detailed a sixteen-hour shift on the Friday before my weekend off and on my way back to the office, close to eleven that night, I was tasked to attend a scene in the lower Shankill Road, Belfast. BRC informed me that I would be briefed by a senior officer from Newry Crime Squad.

When I received this call, I was only about five minutes from the scene; when I got there I was greeted by a familiar face. I had met the officer in charge the previous summer, while we were on holiday in Florida. He oversaw a Crime Squad based in Newry RUC station. The main crime scene was outside the County Down town of Ballynahinch. The house on the Shankill estate is where the proceeds of the crime had been found.

Having seen the items that needed to be removed as evidence, I knew that this would be a mammoth task.

I explained to the SIO that I had been on duty all day and that this was my weekend off, but I was happy to continue working; he was well pleased and so was I. My examination of the scene and subsequent recovery of the items, to Antrim Road RUC station, meant that I did not finish until six on Saturday morning. So just the 23-hour turn, then.

I returned to duty later that Saturday to continue with my examination and again on Sunday morning to finish the task and hand over the exhibits to the designated exhibits officer attached to Newry Crime Squad.

On returning to duty, on Monday, I received a phone call from Maynard thanking me for a job well done. The next phone call I took was from my Detective Inspector, who needed to discuss my F40 overtime figures.

An F40 is a form used by police officers to record the hours worked, including overtime. Those working in the SOCO unit submit their forms to the Detective Inspector at Tennent Street CID, whose office was on the first floor of the station.

On the way to his office, I wondered why there was an issue with my overtime hours, as I had worked them. It was that time of the month again and the forms needed to be signed off and submitted to pay branch, no later than the nineteenth of each month, so that the overtime was included in the following month's salary.

I knocked the office door and entered to be faced by the DI and, siting just behind him, the senior SOCO. The grin on Jim's face would have made the Cheshire Cat jealous. The scene would have made a thinner-skinned person nervous.

One of the attributes that I possess is to think fast and reply fast to whatever is presented to me. On this occasion the DI wanted to know how I had amassed the overtime, as it was my weekend to be off and he was not going to sign for it. I intuitively knew that Jim was the puppet master in this pot-stirring presentation. The grin was still in place.

There was no doubt in my mind that Jim had presented his version of how he would have dealt with the scene in the

Shankill estate, and the length of time involved to complete the task. There was no malice in what he was doing; it was just part of the cut and thrust that one had to keep up with while working in a testosterone-filled environment.

I was not about to justify my actions, so I asked the DI to push over his phone, so that I could make a call. He wanted to know why I needed to use the phone; I told him to bear with me for a moment. The look on Jim's face, at that moment, was quizzical. He could not work out my intention.

The switchboard put me through to the head of Newry Crime Squad, and in his usual gruff tone he asked who was calling. He thanked me once again for my efforts and informed me that the evidence recovered at the Shankill scene had resulted in two arrests. Our conversation lasted around two minutes before he asked me why I had called him.

I told him about my current problem, and he asked me to put the DI on the phone. It was a loud and decidedly one-way conversation. The action taking place in front of me reminded me off the nodding dog ornaments that my uncles had in their cars in the mid-1960s.

Phone call over, I was told to close the office door on my way out. Well, I will leave it up to you to guess if I closed the door.

I have always maintained that fresh air is good for you. I returned to the office and a brief time later Jim entered, minus his grin. I never questioned him about the overtime, as there was no point in kicking someone whose mission had belly flopped. We had a chin wag and a cup of tea before I headed home. All is fair game in love and war. Office politics at its best or as I put it, pure entertainment.

# Chapter 9

## My Friends

If ever there was a case in the history of jurisprudence that represents a thorough ravage of the public purse, the following case qualifies to fly that flag. You have no doubt heard of the phrase 'smoke and mirrors.'

This was a case where the inmates were in charge of the asylum, exercising their ingrained ideology of denial at every juncture.

There were numerous opportunities to resolve this case, but the gravy train was in full flow, unstoppable; and the route it took was planned years in advance, to satisfy the monetary greed of a few individuals.

In the early days of this case some of the players set out to obscure, embellish, and mislead others, to take attention away from what was really at the heart of what had occurred.

For me it was a profoundly disturbing experience from the outset. Initially my friend, Colin, the plaintiff, asked me to review his case.

The incident he was involved in and what followed it was, beyond any doubt, something that altered the course of my friend's life. It was one of the contributing factors that led to his untimely passing.

The following quote from Marcus Tullius Cicero, an orator, lawyer and philosopher, encapsulates this case: 'When you have no basis for an argument, abuse the plaintiff.'

It would take an entire book on its own to describe the legal toing and froing that went on for more than twenty years. However, Colin often told me that he thought the entire process had been a train of copious and unnecessary legal arguments, actions carried out specifically to waste time and drain the public purse.

He believed that the crown was playing the timecard; hoping that his health would deteriorate to such an extent that he would die before getting justice.

Colin told me that he was not concerned about who was involved and what the hidden agenda had been at the time of the incident when a brief gun battle took place outside a Post Office. Once again, he only wanted justice.

On 15<sup>th</sup> September 2016, Colin asked me if I could supply him with a generic report on what examinations should be carried out in connection with the scene in which he had been involved.

 I sent him the following report.

## Fatal shooting at Pomeroy Post Office 28<sup>th</sup> November 1983

In an ideal scenario, where there is no threat to the safety of those engaged in examining the crime scene, the following examination should take place once the scene has been established and secured. The scene should be examined bearing in mind contamination and cross-contamination issues.

- All areas of interest, including potential evidence, should be photographed.
- All areas of interest, including potential evidence, should be mapped.

This scene can be divided into two principal areas as regards a crime scene examination.

- Areas of interest outside the post office including the nearby alley.
- Areas of interest inside the post office.

In respect of the outside scene, which includes the front facade of the post office, one would:

- Note all strike marks on exterior surfaces, made by bullets.
- Recover any ballistic evidence.
- Take glass samples from all broken glass panes.
- Tape lifts of relevant surfaces for fibres.
- Carry out a fingerprint examination on any suitable surfaces.
- Any parked cars of interest should be removed and taken to a more suitable location for later examination. However, if there is anything of importance, having carried out a visual examination, then that item/s should be recovered prior to moving the vehicle.
- The SIO may request that the vehicle/s is examined at the scene (separate SOCO).

- Seize all weapons.

In respect of the scene inside the post office one would:

- Note all strike marks made by bullets.
- Recover any ballistic evidence.
- Fingerprint relevant surfaces.
- Tape lifts of relevant surfaces for fibres.
- Arrange to have the outer clothing of anyone who may have had contact with the culprit/s, seized.
- Take glass samples.
- Recover footwear marks if present.

I am in no doubt that there were several other associated scenes in the investigations   that followed, such as:

- Searches
- Postmortem
- Arrests
- Vehicles

Colin and his section sergeant stated that they had returned fire at a gunman who was standing outside, at the front of the post office, and facing them. If this gunman was in proximity to the front window of the post office, then shattered glass from this window may be on his clothing and footwear.

If this person got into a vehicle wearing the same clothing or changed in a safe house, then there is a possibility of secondary transfer of glass to this vehicle and the house.

Colin compiled a report and sent it to his legal team and to me. I have only made a few corrections to the grammar, which in no way alters the content of his request. This email was sent on 2nd July 2019.

If you read between the lines of this email, you will get an idea of the enormous stress and health-altering issues that this case had caused him. Having spoken to Colin, at length, he always maintained that he and his sergeant were cannon fodder with regards to this incident, in which an innocent lady was killed.


## Subject: Letter to Mrs Justice Keegan/Mrs Chamberlain CSO re current case

**Please forward this email to the above re the 19 years of pre-trial issues in this case.**

The defendant has known, from the outset in 1983, that the Special Branch managed a policing operation involving two of their agents, which resulted in the death of a civilian and injuries including my own.

The liability in the case was directed away from the actions of Special Branch; a uniform sergeant and myself were made the focus of the DPP and Inquest.

The Court directed that my case be included within the PTSD Group Action of 2001. The documentation, now in my possession, clearly indicates that the lead solicitor in my case was acting as an agent for the Crown and colluded with the Crown in ignoring the legal agreements entered before the court and the orders and directions of the court.

This lawyer went to great lengths to assist the Crown in preventing me from forwarding my case. This included providing totally fabricated evidence before a Master and then at appeal.

About 13 years of wasted and fabricated litigation has already taken place at huge cost and a huge amount of the court's time has already been wasted.

The Crown is aware of every aspect of this case and breached National Security by divulging that two agents were directly involved in the case, before Mr Justice Stephens, as he was then.

It is in the public domain that two agents were involved in this SB managed operation. I am also concerned that the Crown has provided the Court with three variations of agent involvement prior to the Closed Measure Procedure taking place, which concerns me greatly. I am aware of the Lord Chief Justice's views on the need for CMPs and the high cost.

It is my belief that, due to national security issues, any possible gist will not contain the exact role these agents played, although it should not be difficult for me to find out.

It is my understanding that the State has a policy of stringing on legacy cases forever, in the hope that people die or just give up. I would like to live long enough to get a fair hearing on the issue, but the Crown appears to want to continue the case, pleading weak and unsustainable issues.

I would respectfully appeal to Ms Chamberlain to consider her role as a solicitor and a custodian of the justice system and to expedite this case before a court of law.

Many of the delays in this case are totally inexcusable.
I believe all of the above issues to be factually correct based on the large amount of documentary evidence I have before me.

Yours faithfully
Colin Keys

In 2022, Colin was awarded damages by a Belfast court as part of a negligence case taken against the PSNI. The damages amounted to £50,000.

There are those who would regard this monetary settlement as substantial. However, whether the payment was substantial should only be decided in relation to the trauma and arduous legal debacle that Colin experienced. In this case the compensation fell well short.

On 28th December 2023 Colin and I met for a pizza and a chin wag. We talked about our families, presents from Santa and our plans for the new year. The two hours passed quickly. We wished each other a happy and healthy 2024 before heading our separate ways once more.

I phoned Colin several times on New Year's Eve but there was no answer. I phoned him again on New Years Day, again no answer. Two days later my phone rang, and it was a mutual friend to tell me that Colin was found dead in his home. He had passed away due to natural causes.

I miss my larger-than-life friend and the time we spent putting the world to rights. I still talk to him, as if he were standing in front of me.

God bless you, Colin.

One meets many people during a lifetime, some are colleagues, some are acquaintances, others are to be ignored, while a few become friends and fewer still become close friends. I want to mention two gentlemen whom I had the pleasure of meeting. When others went out of their way to cause me stress, these men, without hesitation, came to my rescue.

I received an injury on duty in 1981, which resulted in back surgery, followed by a considerable time off work. Prior to returning to duty, I was assessed by a doctor attached to the Occupational Health Unit, based in Seapark, Carrickfergus.

The doctor who examined me was, at that time, my neighbour. He told me that it was the intention of my pay master's to terminate my employment, and he asked me what

I thought about this turn of events. It will not come as a surprise to you to hear that my response was quite vivid.

Having listened to my retort the doctor agreed with my views, and so he recommended that I was fit to return to duty. This was a case where those who held the power had played their cards, without empathy, but the OHU doctor played a better hand. I went on to have a full career in the police.

This was not the first time that some of the white shirts had tried to cause my family and me stress. I often wonder why someone would go out of their way to cause hardship to another person, when there are no grounds to support their actions.

It is my view that the personalities of these so-called colleagues fall under the heading of sociopathy and psychopathy. Such people, with their agendas, lack empathy, sympathy, and compassion. I was tempted to include apathy but on reflection it is clear they do not lack motivation in striving to obtain their goals.

This story is a personal example of what happens when a regular person comes up against a wall of sociopathy.

I stepped out of the bath and trapped the sciatic nerve in my lower back, in the area where I had the surgery in 1981. For those of you who suffer from bouts of sciatica, you can understand the level of pain and disability involved. For those of you who have never experienced this pain, I confess I am extremely envious of you; and I sincerely hope that you never experience it.

Despite medication, light exercise, rest and several sessions of physiotherapy, the pain persisted. I contacted my doctor followed by my private health insurance company, and an MRI scan followed. Due to the findings of this scan, I arranged an appointment with an orthopaedic surgeon called John Nixon.

Mr Nixon advised me to suffer for as long as I could. He gave me his private telephone number and said that when I could suffer no longer, I was to phone him. During this time, I took oral pain medication, along with periodic injections of morphine administered by a doctor. I am blessed with a high pain threshold, so I lasted from late March to early July before I made the call.

I phoned John Nixon on a Sunday morning. Unfortunately, he told me that he could not fit me in for an operation the following week, as he was extremely busy; but then he told me that he would call a colleague, who in turn would phone me. Several hours passed and then his friend phoned me, a Mr Ian Adair. Mr Adair asked me if I could be in Musgrave Park Hospital, for seven on Thursday morning; he would talk me through the procedure, and I would be on the table around eight. I of course could not wait.

He was honest and upfront, telling me that the procedure only had a 50/50 chance of being a total success. I was past caring. I simply said, 'Let's get this done.' The operation went well but the recovery period was long and arduous. Several of my SOCO colleagues called to see me; but not one senior officer called until I was almost six months into my recovery.

The doorbell sounded and my wife answered the door. It was a senior officer who now oversaw the day-to-day running of SOCO, as the structure of the unit had changed. My wife ushered him into the living room. I was sitting in a highchair provided by occupational health via my GP.

It did not take him long before he showed his true colours. He never asked me how I was coping or anything to do with my welfare. The main objective of his visit was to get my signature on a form. Before I put pen to paper I asked him the purpose of this form.

He had not brought flowers or chocolate, so I was quite sure he was not there for the good of my health, and I was correct. He had door stepped me to inform me that since I had been off work for six months, I would now be going onto half pay, as per force instructions. They say timing is the secret of good comedy but there was nothing funny about this move. It was now mid-October, with two days to go before my F40 needed to be submitted to pay branch.

I explained to him that my second back operation was medically linked to my injury on duty back in 1981; but he just ignored my explanation. I could see that there was something going on behind his presented facade.

In such medically linked cases one does not go onto half pay. However, to get this sociopath out of my home I signed the form, and my wife showed him the door. His farewell was no more heartfelt than our greeting.

This whole debacle had caused me a lot of unnecessary stress. I needed to think fast; this was the Christmas pay that he was going to have reduced. I knew the gentleman to call.

I asked my wife to lift the chair into the hall beside the phone, as I needed to contact Welfare Branch. This unit was based in Lisnasharragh RUC Station, Belfast and this member of staff had helped me in the past with work-related stress and bereavement. I cannot speak highly enough of George, and for what he has done for me and my family.

I spoke with George and several hours later he phoned back to tell me that he had sorted the matter. He also told me to try and ignore my erstwhile visitor, who did not have my welfare at heart. George had phoned Mr Adair's personal secretary, outlining the facts. Mr Adair, consultant orthopaedic surgeon, penned a report on my behalf stating that the current disc prolapse, in my back, was related to the 1981 injury and everything was faxed to pay branch. I was not put on half pay. George and I met several times during my career, and I regard him as a friend. If only we had more people like George in our lives.

During the week that I returned to work, the person who tried to interfere with my Christmas list remarked, 'Well, I see that you got the issue sorted.' I took George's advice and ignored him.

I have another friend who stopped me from drowning in my own thoughts. His name was Jim. This gentleman and former colleague had a skill that few have, and a heart to match. It is almost ten years since his passing, as I sit here looking at his image on the order of service, which takes pride of place beside my computer.

My wife had noticed that I was going through a personality change, and my daughters agreed. I thought that everything in the garden was rosy, but when the issues were laid bare for me, the penny dropped. However, it took a while for me to accept that I needed help. One day, as I was walking into the police complex known as Maryfield, located in Holywood, Belfast, I saw Jim talking to my sister-in-law. I continued and got on with my business. At this point Jim and Jenny were standing on the steps, outside the main door, and they were still deep in conversation. I acknowledged their presence again and walked towards the car. I had only taken a few steps when Jenny said, 'This is the man you need to speak to.' I stopped and turned back.

She had probably already talked to Jim about her favourite brother-in-law. Jenny left, and it was my intention to follow when Jim told me that it was his lunch time, and would I like to join him in his office? I accepted this invitation and what began on that day continued until three months before his passing.

So, what did Jim do for me? Well, what he did for me — and my close family — was to put my life back on track. The process was spread out over several years; inevitably I got derailed, from time to time.

Jim sustained life-changing injuries as the result of a terrorist incident, perpetrated by the Provisional IRA. His injuries were such that he accepted a medical retirement. He had entered the RUC through the RUC cadet scheme, and he was in the original corps of cadets who went to Hendon Police College, London. I was to be in the second group, but you know that sad story already.

During the next few years, he studied and after demanding work he qualified as an expert counsellor, specialising in trauma. He had worked in a trauma laden environment for years and had been a victim of trauma; thus, he was ideally placed to help others cope. His skills were not confined to serving and retired police officers in Northern Ireland, either.

His unique service was heavily in demand throughout the UK and beyond, an example being working with survivors of the war in Bosnia. But what I know best about Jim is how he helped me cope. My sessions took place in three locations over the years: his office, his home, and my home.

Due to funding and the system in place, I was allocated only a set number of sessions in the Maryfield complex, which was his official place of employment. Most of our sessions took place in our homes, where we discussed everything and anything. I did all the talking while Jim listened.

During one of these sessions my daughter asked him if he would like a slice of her Victoria sponge. He accepted this offer with the proviso that his wife was never to hear about it. He needed to watch his sugar levels. Gradually, this became a regular ritual in our house but luckily for his health, as he knew in advance what was being offered, he was able to adjust his daily calorie consumption accordingly.

I asked him did he ever tell his wife M about the bun eating, and he smiled enigmatically, which I took to be a no.

Jim gave up his free time to help me cope; I mean, he gave up a lot of time. Or perhaps he only came for the Victoria sponge. From time to time, I bought him items I thought might be useful for him; I also power hosed his drive, which he was not able to do due to his injuries.

There are many people walking around today, with a good headspace, thanks to my friend Jim, and that includes me. His remains are buried in a cemetery near my home, and I visit his grave from time to time to seek solace.

I miss him. God bless you, my friend.

Another friend who is dear to my heart is from an area of North Africa known as the Maghreb. He had nine siblings and from an early age he wanted to be a police officer. His ethnic background was a mix of Berber, Arab and French. He has an infectious personality and without hesitation I can vouch that he can talk for a considerable time on a single inhalation. So how did he become an officer in what was the greatest police force in the world before it was resigned to the annals of history?

Growing up in an environment rich in diversity moulded him into the person he is today. His parents worked hard to provide for their children, bringing them up so that they could face the world, when the time was right. He left home at the age of eighteen and moved to France, where he worked in various jobs. Being fluent in French, Arabic and English gave him a big advantage and he was never short of work.

During his time in France, he met a young lady from Northern Ireland. She was in France for a year as a foreign language student, while studying for a degree at Queens University Belfast. The year together passed quickly, and their relationship grew stronger. When it was time for her to return home to Northern Ireland, Johnnie realised he had to plan. He decided to join her a few weeks later.

Unsure, at first, what he could do in his adopted country, he decided to go to university, where he studied so that he would be able to teach French as a career. He taught French for a while; then he moved jobs and managed a bookshop. So, did he marry the lady that he met in France? Of course he did. They could now argue fluently, in two languages, should the occasion arise; assuming the poor woman could get a word in edgeways.

Despite having an excellent job, his dream of becoming a police officer was still alive in the background. There was a recruitment drive in February 1982, and with his new British passport in hand he applied to join the Royal Ulster Constabulary. He was successful in his application and in March 1982 he entered the RUC training centre in Enniskillen, County Fermanagh. When he retired from the police, his skills in speaking French and Arabic were put to effective use by another employer (one with a lower public profile) who recruited him.

Now, look; I do not want you people, who are probably all on Facebook and have thousands of friends, to think that I only have four of them. Thankfully, I have many more and we meet from time to time. Sometimes I forget whose turn it is to pay the bill. However, the sharper wits are always there to remind me. I blame it on too much caffeine.

My best friend is my wife and that goes without saying.

# Chapter 10

# Working Together or Not Working Together

It is crucial that the investigators and the CSIs work as a team during any major incident so that the best possible outcome can be achieved. The following is a list of protocols that need to be followed.

**Scene Strategy**

The management of a crime scene will impact on the quality, quantity and integrity of the material gathered. The identification of a crime scene is, therefore, a priority for the investigator as it may contain vital material which could influence the outcome of the investigation.

Once investigators have identified a scene, they should apply the investigative mindset to make an initial assessment of its potential to provide evidential material. This assessment and the subsequent formulation of a scene strategy should have due regard to forensic considerations. Undue delay or failure to consider forensic issues at this stage may lead to valuable material being contaminated, overlooked, or lost.

283

The extent to which investigators are responsible for managing a crime scene and developing crime scene strategies is influenced by the complexity or seriousness of the investigation.

When gathering the material, investigators should consult with CSI's and Crime Scene Managers (CSM) to ensure that they use the most appropriate method of evidence recovery.

**IDENTIFYING SCENES**

The crime scene can present itself in several ways and may not be immediately obvious to the investigator or initial attending officers. This may include:

- The victim.
- Witnesses.
- Routes to and from the scene.
- The suspect.
- Weapons (including live and spent ammunition).
- Bomb making materials.
- The suspect's home address or other premises.
- Vehicles (including boats and caravans).
- Dump sites (including victims, clothing, weapons, or stolen property).

Often the scene of the offence will be relatively easy to identify and should, therefore, be considered a fast-track action (see Initial Investigation). The victim, or witnesses to the offence, may be able to tell investigators precisely where and how the offence was committed. This will enable investigators to preserve the scene at the earliest opportunity and to recover the best possible material in a manner which preserves its integrity. However, the investigator should bear in mind that the boundary of the scene may change if new information becomes available.

**Securing Scenes**

The purpose of securing a scene is to maintain the integrity and provenance of any material which may be recovered from it. This simple and important action will reduce the opportunities for the material to become contaminated or inadvertently cross-contaminated.

Anyone who enters the scene has the potential to take something of the scene with them or leave something of themselves behind. This means that every contact has the potential to leave a trace, however miniscule. Such traces are usually:

- Fingerprints.

- DNA.
- Fibres.
- Footwear marks.

These traces provide valuable material that can link a suspect to the crime. The techniques for recovering this material are highly specialised and CSI's have the necessary training and equipment to carry them out.

**Methods Used to Secure a Crime Scene**

There are several methods that the investigator can use to secure and manage crime scenes. These include:

- Using tape to establish an outer and inner cordon, thus securing access to or from the scene.
- Deploying officers to guard the boundaries of the scene (bearing in mind potential cross-contamination issues).
- Roadblocks to protect wider scenes.
- Temporary fencing to keep members of the public and press at a safe distance.
- Ensuring that people entering the stage are wearing suitable protective clothing to prevent contamination

of the scene and to ensure that they are protected from any hazards present.

- Logging full details of all the people who enter and leave the scene.

The investigator should seek advice from CSM's or CSI's or other suitably qualified experts to determine the appropriate level and method of protection required. This may include covering or lighting areas of the scene to protect potential evidence.

**Risks to the scene which must be managed include:**

- Contamination of the scene by items being taken into or from the scene, or cross- contamination by transference between scenes.
- Damage being caused to the scene or material by exposure to the elements.
- Damage to the evidence by insecure structures (the safety of those entering the scene is paramount).
- Microbiological activity causes decay to material.
- Animal disturbance.
- The effect of time delay on certain material types.

## Scene Examination

Once a crime scene has been located and preserved, the recovery of all material should only be undertaken by an individual who is trained to perform this role. In some crime investigations this may be the initial investigator, CSI, or other forensic specialist. If an investigator has any doubts regarding appropriate recovery and preservation techniques, they should obtain advice from a CSI or Crime Scene Manager (CSM).

Scenes should be examined using a structured approach determined by the parameters and requirements of the investigation. It is important that the investigator **communicates** with the person examining the crime scene as the investigation progresses. It is important that this **communication** is a two-way flow between the investigator and the CSI, as to how the scene examination is progressing. This should be specific where required, but flexible enough to allow the facts to become apparent through methodical examination techniques. The scene strategy should be developed in consultation with the forensic scientist, the Senior Investigating Officer (SIO/Prosecutor) and the CSM.

The investigator must be conversant with all material that

has been recovered from the scene. They need to recognise why it has recovered and its potential evidential value. In general crime investigations this may only amount to a few items or exhibits. Advice and guidance regarding issues of contamination, cross-contamination, continuity, exhibit handling, transportation and storage can be obtained from CSM's. Investigators should be aware of the information a forensic examination can provide. This includes confirming or eliminating the presence of the following at a crime scene or other location:

- Victim(s).

- Suspect(s)/Offenders.

- Weapon(s).

- Substance(s).

- Other object(s).

This is achieved by identifying a range of items:

- Physical (fingerprints, footwear marks, tool marks or fibres).

- Biological (blood, semen, saliva, or head hair).

- Chemical (drugs).

- Other substances (firearms discharge residue, glass, petroleum) in or on a crime scene or individual.

Investigators must also understand the present limits of scientific examinations, i.e., what they **cannot** achieve.

Further information which investigators should consider includes:

- Prioritising the order of recovery of physical material (e.g., blood, fingerprints, hairs, fibres, fluids, and documents).

- Ensuring the integrity of all scenes and preventing cross-contamination.

- The need for and frequency of crime scene conferences.

- Which scene should be given priority in multi-scene investigations?

Establishing who has examining precedence at the scene e.g., CSI, pathologist, biologist, fire investigator or forensic scientists. This must be coordinated by the SIO, CSM and Lead Forensic Scientist. The SIO will maintain overall responsibility for deciding the order of precedence.

The use of a forensic strategy will enable the investigator to maximise the potential of any material recovered during the crime scene examination phase.

The following range of investigative options can be developed by using forensic examination. They are equally applicable to any investigation.

**Forensic Strategy**

- Clarification of the circumstances – providing movements of victims and suspects, establishing crime scenes and attack sites, and challenging assumptions.
- Elimination of suspects – through DNA or finger/palm prints.
- Forensic intelligence – providing potential links from scene to suspect and scene to scene, through material recovered.
- Recovered evidence – the identification of an unknown person or fact, for example, identification

through fingerprints or via DNA deposits.

- Context – once the evidence has been obtained, establishing where it fits in the context of the whole investigation or examinations.
- Clarification of the sequence of events – through, for example, analysis of blood distribution, footwear pattern analysis or the use of fire investigation units.
- Corroboration – including independent confirmation of circumstances, critical fact or witness testimony and evidence of the culpability of a suspect.

The use of forensics may also provide the investigator with information that can be used during interviews to assess the reliability of an account. It may also assist them in prioritising lines of enquiry or submitting items for examination at an early stage.

The investigator should carefully examine forensic results to determine their meaning. If the significance of the information cannot be established, they should seek advice and clarification from a CSM and forensic scientist.

In serious or complex investigations, the number of items or exhibits may be substantial and will require the appointment of an exhibits officer.

The exhibits officer's responsibilities include liaison with CSI's and CSM's to ensure that the recovery, handling, storage, and submission of all relevant exhibits are undertaken. The exhibits officer must maintain a close working relationship with the investigating officer to ensure that they are aware of all developments in the investigation.

In addition, information concerning submissions and the results of forensic examinations should be brought to the investigating officer's attention.

Additional advice and assistance can be obtained from CSI's and CSM's.

The success of any investigation is dependent on the quality of material that is obtained from the scene, victims, witnesses, and suspects. A major source of material in police investigations comes from interviews with victims and witnesses. This should be accurate and in as much detail as possible as information provided by witnesses and victims can help to validate or challenge a suspect's version of events.

For those of you who have never seen the after math of a bomb scene on the streets of Northern Ireland, other than on the television, the following photograph is to let you see the complexity of such a scene. The CID investigation into such an event is also complex and by working together progress is possible.

This was a substantial bomb scene and thankfully nobody was killed, and nobody was severely injured. The debris was spread everywhere, so it was a complex scene with regard to recovering the evidence.

Two of the mortars launched successfully while the third detonated inside the vehicle. It was a long day in the field. How can such an incident be filed away under the heading of The Troubles? What nonsense.

The remains of the vehicle that contained the devices are straddling the wall.

For the uninitiated where would you begin if faced with this scene.

Pieces of the bomb timer.

I was pleasantly sidetracked for a time during one of my short breaks. On this occasion I was standing inside the cordon when a dark green-coloured Jaguar car pulled up, on the roadside, and two gentlemen stepped out.

They were dressed in their Sunday best, and it was only Saturday. One stood outside the car while the other walked over to me but remained outside the cordon. I knew both good men. I had been to several bomb scenes where they were in charge of making the scenes safe, so that I could conduct my examinations.

The chap at the car was the Senior Army Technical Officer, SATO. I shouted over to him remarking that he had lost weight since we last met. His reply was colourful. The other chap was a Captain in the same unit. They were on their way to meet some dignitaries and needed a comprehensive briefing of what had taken place.

I met the captain some weeks later and I asked him if the interrogation went well. The penny dropped straight away, and he looked me in the eye and replied, "thank goodness we stopped to talk to you." I met this officer and his colleagues several times socially. On one occasion, while staying on the army base, I woke up to find his Irish Wolfhound lying on top of the bed at my back.

The following legal case is an example of **not working together** to reach an honest outcome.

We met as a group of friends to consider this issue and here is the result of our considerations which were penned by our friend. I am in receipt of an injury on duty pension based on my physical and mental health conditions. Choosing to go down the injury on duty route was my choice rather than commence a legal action that would have taken years to conclude, bringing with it more stress and anxiety.

Below you will find the detail of this saga. It is quite extraordinary. A legal issue [or set of issues] that could have been decided by a "test case" was instead the scene of a protracted, intricate, and hugely costly "group action" for all involved.

The gravy train had pulled into the station, with a full load, once again, and needed to be lightened of its load. The outcome was a partial victory for the police officers. It opened the door for action in individual cases within established parameters.

The press universally painted it as a defeat for police and a victory for the Chief Constable. Over five thousand officers melted away. Just a few hardy souls persisted. What became of the others, their condition, and if they received any treatment is unknown. The Police Federation were asked for their comments, but they did not reply.

An organisation that has as much cash in the bank as the Police Federation might have been expected to fund deserving cases, on the basis that the costs would be recouped. The scandal can be firmly laid at the door of the Police Federation, for its failure to accurately assess, control, manage, fund, and protect the interests of its members. The only winners were the lawyers.

Police officers in Northern Ireland started a 'group action' against their employer about the issue of diagnosis and treatment of mental issues such as post-traumatic stress disorder.

Leaving aside the wisdom of such an action, when a test case or two could have potentially produced the same result; it was funded by the Police Federation, a statutory body, which in the presence of a ban on police officers joining a trade union, serves as their representative body.

Membership of the PF is free to all officers. To obtain additional benefits, such as legal assistance, officers are required to pay a subscription. Four officers are elected to be the full-time representatives, and they receive a two-rank enhancement in pay. A constable elected as a full time official will receive an inspector's salary, including pension. At the end of 2016, the PF had assets more than eight million pounds.

In his judgment, delivered in 2007, Coghlin J said the following:

[3] *While the litigation has tended to focus upon the disorder known as post-traumatic stress disorder ("PTSD") the claims also encompass other conditions such as depression, anxiety and adjustment reactions or disorders.*

Coghlin's judgment was complex, and both parties appealed certain issues to the Court of Appeal.

Girvan LJ, in a judgment dealt with grounds 1 and 4 of the respondent's appeal, namely, the duty to provide training, education and/or information including stress awareness training. In light of his conclusions, with which the other members of the court agreed, that the respondent's failure to provide training and education was not a breach of the defendant's duty of care to individual plaintiffs, it was no longer necessary to consider grounds 2 and 5 (the extent to which, if at all, and the respects in which the respondent was in breach of any duty of care in failing to provide training, education and/or information).

In short, The Court of Appeal said:

*The remainder of the judgment therefore deals with the single outstanding issue – that of the alleged duty to treat (ground 7). Before turning to that issue, however, it is necessary to say something about a subject which occupied not a little time on the hearing of the appeal viz the approach that this court should take to findings of fact made by the trial judge.*

*[45]    It is apparent that initially OHU was not seen as a facility for the treatment of psychological or psychiatric illnesses, at least in the case of more significant conditions. This is unsurprising.*

*[57]    **What makes the position of RUC members unique, at least in recent UK history, is that they have been a force exposed on a regular basis to a level of trauma not experienced elsewhere**. At the time that treatment (as well as diagnosis) of psychiatric and psychological problems within the RUC was being undertaken, the respondent was being told by his OHU team of the inadequacies of referrals to outside agencies. A stark dilemma was presented to him. Should those who were at*

*risk of developing these conditions (or, even worse, had already suffered from them) be further exposed to circumstances that would either precipitate or exacerbate those problems without the prospect of adequate treatment or should he ensure that treatment was available from the resources of the force itself?* **We consider that a blanket exemption from a duty to treat cannot in those circumstances be justified.**

*[59]     The police officers' appeal on the question of the question of resources is dismissed for the reasons earlier given in this judgment. The Chief Constable's appeal on the question of training, information and education is allowed to the extent that is defined in Girvan LJ's judgment. The appeal in relation to the question whether the respondent was in fact in breach of that duty is no longer relevant.* **The Chief Constable's appeal in relation to the duty to treat is dismissed.**

## Background of the litigation

The solicitors in the case was Edwards and Co. This firm had an agreement with the PF that it would handle a substantial portion of their claims in Northern Ireland.

The PTSD action was only one of many cases it handled.

The spend of costs in this case is significant. Bear in mind what the Court of Appeal said about evidence presented by the group action in the trial regarding the operation of the RUC Occupational health.

*Such evidence as was given on this topic on behalf of the plaintiffs was remarkably slight.*

How could this be when the original cases with Bogue & McNulty Solicitors contained complex issues, with regards to mental health.

Consider then, the fees claimed from the PF by Edwards and Company at various stages in the action. Before doing so you should know that there are potentially three distinct areas of claim.

## Outlay

This would cover a multitude of areas such as photocopying, but it could also cover payments to experts.

## Solicitor costs

These are almost always agreed in advance. A partner solicitor will be entitled to a greater hourly fee than a non-partner, and then a paralegal will charge less, then, at the bottom of the list will be the humble clerk. The fact that the client is charged these sums does not mean that the person receives them. The money goes into the coffers of the solicitor's firm and each person receives his salary or, in the case of a partner, potentially a salary plus profit share.

## Counsel costs

Generally, counsel agrees a brief fee plus refreshers. This means that, on completion of the case, the barrister gets the brief fee and an extra fee for each day he spent in court. Usually, these payments are claimed on the finalisation of the case.

Sometimes, in a complex case, an hourly rate may be negotiated with counsel, to be paid on a monthly or other regular basis. In those circumstances a brief fee may or may not be claimed. Of course, all of this should be agreed in advance with the client, the PF who will ultimately foot the bill.

So, let us look at some costs.

In the quarter July to September 2005 Edwards and Co claimed that they had spent £469,757.26 on behalf of the police officers. The individual bills came to £89.05 for every officer.

**Senior Counsel claimed £131,000 for this three-month period**. At that time, the Serious Fraud Office, which handles the most difficult white-collar crime in the United Kingdom, was not paying senior counsel much more than £100.00 per hour. So, he must have worked about 1,300 hours in the period July to September 2005. Perhaps the PF was paying him well above the going rate.

There cannot have been much court time if any. Three months is about ninety days. It works out at **£1455.00 per day**, if he worked every day and did not take any holidays.

But he also had some help.

**First barrister; claimed £49,550.00 for the same period, or £550 for every day, July to the end of September.**

**Second, barrister; claimed £40,000. A slightly lower daily rate of £444 for every day.**

**So, beavering away for the PF and their 5,500 members, three counsel cost them just over £220,000 for three months.**

What did they get in return?

**But we are not finished. In the period January to March 2006, Edwards and Co claimed over £600,000. Three barristers claimed: £150,000, £39,000, and £34,000, respectfully. A total for ninety days of £224,000 or roughly £2,500 per day.**

**In the next quarter, April-June 2006 the three legal friends claimed: £209,000, £150,000, and £140,000, respectfully. Total almost £500k. One barrister also claimed for a Value Cabs fare of £16.80.**

Police officers suffering from PTSD might wonder what those sums were spent on.

The three sets of accounts that have been quoted are also replete with mention of many experts, more than ten.

Astonishing that eventually the trial heard such a paucity of expert evidence.

So, what was the final bill for PTSD? How much did the PF pay Edwards? How much was paid directly to Edwards by police officers and what costs, if any, were paid to the Chief Constable?

Here is what is known.

Up to August 2003 Edwards had received £1,000,000 for "generic work".

**Bill for July –September 2005**        **£469,757**

**Bill for January –March 2006**        **£600,993**

**Bill for April –June 2006**        **£844,852**

We do not have all the bills but even this snippet suggests that the total bill presented to the PF by Edwards and Co was more than £3,000,000.

What is also known is that in 2015, the PF paid out £1,000,000 in "PTSD final settlement". Where this money went is not stated. It is referred to in the foreword to the accounts as "the settlement of the costs in the long running Post Traumatic Stress Disorder legal case, which resulted in an outflow from the Fund of £1 million." Why did it take six years after the end of the case to settle this bill?

<u>Aftermath of the litigation</u>

First, the decision of the Court of Appeal did not close the door on 5,500 officers' claims.

Second, the **PF declined to further fund these claims.**

Third; officers were entitled to pursue individual claims and many considered doing so. They were met with warnings from the Chief Constable's lawyers about the legal costs involved, should their claims fail. Consequently, only a handful of officers have pursued claims.

Fourth; the decisions of Coghlin J. and the Court of Appeal had no bearing on an entirely different type of case. That where the officer developed PTSD or another mental health issue because of a failure to act or a deliberate act on the part of the Chief Constable, in or about a specific event.

The Courts accept that the duties of a police officer in NI during the Troubles resulted in almost daily exposure to danger. But many officers say that they were put in harm's way by the activities of, for example, the Special Branch.

Take the following example. A specialist police unit know that a robbery of a post office will take place at a time and place. The robbery will be carried out by armed terrorists. This unit decides not to inform uniform branch.

The robbery takes place, a civilian is shot during a firefight between uniformed police and terrorists. An officer subsequently develops PTSD. His claim is based on the duty of his employer, the Chief Constable, to take care of his employee.

In September 2009 Edwards & Company wrote to members of the "PTSD Group Action", stating, correctly, that despite media reports to the contrary, neither side achieved a 'knock out' victory. It was clear that the PF was unwilling to fund further cases and therefore they proposed to produce a 'toolkit' which individual officers could use to mount their own claims.

The toolkit was duly produced, and it contained all the necessary forms and guidance for acting in either the High Court or the County Court.

Thus, irrespective of the action or inaction of the PF, each member of the group action appears to have been told, plainly by Edwards and Co, that their case was not lost. They had the option of continuing, albeit without any financial support from the PF. Hence the 'toolkit.'

Only a handful of officers pursued this avenue. It is unclear why. Whilst the potential costs of a lost High Court case were off-putting, costs in the County Court were more manageable. However, this option was not stressed in any way. This would have been the option to take.

So, what was going on within the PF? My friend met with two members of the PF committee in February 2018. This is what they told him.

The initial impetus for the group action came from the PF. It may be that Bogue and McNulty got the thing up and running on a commercial basis, and then Edwards and Co became involved.

Counsel's opinion was not obtained until some way down the line. The PF committee was aware of bills coming in from Edwards and Co. There is no evidence that any controls were placed on spending.

There is a suggestion that the PF committee told their members that the case was lost [by word of mouth] and that nothing more could be done. This contrasts with the 'toolkit' which set out the position with admirable clarity.

## Conclusion

Regarding the representation of officers by the lead solicitors Edwards and Co., one must question the wisdom of pursuing a "group action" but, given that I am not privy to the advice of counsel or the twists and turns of the case, I am not in a position to give any view, except to express surprise. These actions are normally used where each Plaintiff has the same complaint. For example, an inherent defect in an electrical appliance.

In respect of the running of the case, again, I have no knowledge base, therefore I cannot comment, save to highlight the sums expended and the Court of Appeal's comment on the paucity of expert evidence.

What is more troublesome is the role played by the PF in instigating, funding, and abandoning the litigation.

Each officer would have had two basic relationships. One with the PF and the second with a lawyer, whether Edwards or Bogue and McNulty. I have already commented on the lawyer aspects.

Regarding an officer's relationship with the PF, first it has a statutory duty to represent officers, whether they make any payment to the PF. That duty relates to the officer's relationship with the Chief Constable. Second, those officers who made a payment would appear to be in a contractual relationship over and above the statutory relationship with the PF. I am not in possession of any terms and conditions.

It may or may not be that, in taking the claim in the first place, in failing to control costs and the management of the action during the course of the action, and in failing to pursue or help to pursue an officer's claims, post the Court of Appeal decision, the PF may or may not have been in breach of contract with each and every officer.

Like the Grand Old Duke of York, the PF led 5,500 members up the extremely expensive hill of 'group litigation'. Having won a victory, **regarding duty to treat**, it then led them down again and left them to their own choices.

The following matter revolved around office politics and the restructuring of what was always considered as a role that only police officers could carry out.

Decisions had been made, by those holding the purse strings, to employ civilians as SOCO personnel once their training was successfully completed.

As many of you know change is inevitable. So, you either embrace change or place obstacles in its path. It is the passing of time that lets one see if change has worked or failed. There were considerable in-house conversations between my colleagues regarding how this change would affect our position. Would we be phased out, transferred back to uniform immediately, or offered early retirement?

We were left in limbo by management for a considerable time, as civilianisation carried on. No change there then! So, here we were dealing with horrific sights and now being hammered by our own side. However, once again we just carried on regardless despite the pressure.

On a personal basis I embraced the change with open arms. However, others did not. I had been in SOCO about 2 years when I was asked if I would be willing to take on a new partner for 3 months. I was to observe the working practices of this civilian SOCO, from a border division, and compile a report on him without his knowledge.

I allowed this idea to occupy my thoughts for about 10 seconds before responding. I needed to know why this so-called covert action was needed and why me. I was told that it was an order from on high. I had no choice but to run with this, but I was determined to find out why this was happening. I smelt a rat.

The following week my new partner walked into the office and after introductions I brought him to the canteen for a friendly chat and away from the hearing of others. After swapping spit for around 10 minutes, I had the measure of the man.

This is not his name but for continuity reasons I will call him, John. By the end of our first day, working together, I had his character nailed. By the end of our first week, working together, I had his working practices nailed.

From our conversations I put 2 and 2 together, which revealed to me why he had been sent to our office. It was a case of change and office politics involving his two police colleagues.

Now and again some of my schoolteachers penned this comment to my end of term report, 'could have done better.' For me John could not have done any better. I gave him gold stars throughout his tenure as my temporary partner.

John, for me, was a valuable colleague and we worked together numerous times during the years that followed. He had served his country, for many years, before becoming a SOCO and served it again in a civilian capacity.

Our paths crossed recently and during this tête-à-tête I told him about my report, of which he had no idea. We just smiled at the absurdity of it. Just to let you know it was several years before we were told that we could remain in post as a police SOCO, until retirement.

# Chapter 11

# My Irish Roots

My paternal great grandmother was born in Cork, Ireland, which is in the province of Munster. For those of you who have never seen this area of Ireland, it is worth a visit. I have visited this region of south-west Ireland several times over the years.

This diligent lady moved to Dublin, in her youth, where she met my great grandfather; things happened as they do, and they married a brief time later. It did not take long before their first child was born, followed by fourteen more (but those were the days) before they called time on making babies.

One of these children became my grandmother, after she met and married a County Fermanagh man who had decided to take a holiday in Dublin. They raised ten children while residing in Belfast.

My grandmother never lost her south Dublin lilt throughout her lifetime. I loved the softness in her voice. She was the only family member who moved away from their south Dublin farms.

My mum and dad would drive to Dublin, at least twice a year, so that my grandmother could spend time with her family. We stayed for one or two weeks, usually during our school holidays. I stayed in what was known locally as the 'big house.' This was the home of my great aunt, my grandmother's younger sister. I had almost free reign as my mum, dad and grandmother stayed at one of the home farms, some two miles away.

My great aunt kept pigs, chickens and sometimes horses, as one of her sons was a jockey. When he retired from his time in the saddle he became a horse trainer with stables in Newbridge, County Kildare.

Now and then she would butcher a pig for the family table and dispatch a chicken or two for the pot. In case you are of a nervous – or vegan – disposition, I will leave it up to your imagination as to how this was achieved. I was present at one such event when I was about twelve years old. My job was to hold a large bowl while the pig's tongue, feet, parts of the head and heart were placed in it. Little of the pig was wasted.

So, there I was holding a bowl full of pig parts and wondering what comes next. Have you ever heard of brawn? I had no idea what this was until my great aunt took the bowl from me and asked me to follow her into the scullery, where she prepared the piggy delights before making brawn. All the parts were cooked, chopped up, mixed with spices, and placed in a mould, before aspic was poured over the mix. Once set, this terrine style dish was ready to be sliced and gratefully eaten.

Well, did I taste it? My great aunt assured me that I would like it, and she was right. I was hesitant in the beginning, but if it were available during my visits to her home, I would have a brawn sandwich. I do not know if it is available today but if it is, please taste it. Oh; I almost forgot. My other job was to pluck the chickens. Dead chickens that is. Sorry another dad joke.

Now the 'big house' was flanked on the left by a Garda station and the next building was a pub. On the opposite flank there was another pub. This police station was manned by one Garda officer, who also slept in the place. This officer of the

317

law would often call in with my great aunt and uncle to take tea and have a chinwag.

On some occasions he would partake in a glass of John Power whisky. My great uncle was fond of this brand of whisky. When I stayed with him, he would often ask me to go across to Larry, the pub owner, and get him a baby Power. This was a small bottle of whiskey that contained one measure. He drank the contents neat, filled the bottle with water and drank the water some ten minutes later. I did between four and six whiskey runs a day.

Sometimes the whiskey run was undertaken before the pub opened. I would knock on the side door, which Larry opened, and follow him into the lounge bar, where he would hand me the small bottle. No money ever changed hands during my stays.

My great uncle did work on Larry's cars. I do not know if he charged his friend for the work, but what I can tell you is that my great uncle had a large thirst. When I was old enough, I would frequent these hostelries with my family.

There was a fantastic community atmosphere in this small village, which offered me the chance to taste beer in a public house aged fifteen. This may seem young, but it was not my first encounter with beer.

On a Saturday night another great uncle would play poker, in the parlour, with his brothers and my dad. It was during one of those games that my great uncle let me drink some of his beer, which I watched him pour from a small bottle. It was called McArdle's Ale, and I was twelve. I also got the chance, when my mother was not looking, to sup a little beer during family wakes, which always took place at one of the home farms. I was present at three wakes during my teenage years.

For those of you who have never been present at an Irish wake, let me paint you a picture of what takes place. The deceased is washed, dressed in their Sunday best and placed face up on the bed, in a position of repose. I saw two of my great uncles in this position, while a third was in his open coffin. I remember asking my father about the coins on their eyes and he told me that they were placed there just in case the eyelids popped opened. Could you imagine the shock of seeing the eyelids pop open as you were leaning over the body to say your goodbyes?

The wake usually takes place during the days (a brief period; the Irish are traditionally quick to bury their dead) between the death and the funeral. During this period of mourning family and friends would call in to pay their respects. Those calling at the house would bring copious amounts of homemade food, along with drink to wash it down. It is a traditional social event to honour the life of the deceased. One could even describe it as a party for the deceased.

Some remarkable stories emerged from family members, the minister, and the priest. I was young at the time, but I remember a story that my grandmother told to those gathered around the fire.

The lights were turned off, leaving the glow of the fire as the only source of light. As the flames rose, casting our shadows across the room, there was a deathly silence until the story began. Her version of the story, about a female spirit in Irish folklore known as the Banshee (the Banshee; the white fairy woman), scared the bejesus out of me. I could not sleep for days.

She told us that, as a young girl she saw the Banshee crossing the field behind where we were seated and the following day her father, who was ill at the time, passed away. My grandmother would always stay for a few days after a family funeral, during which time there would be further get-togethers to celebrate the life of the deceased.

Now back to my great uncle.

I would stay at his home, the odd time, where I was given an important task. He had several oak barrels that contained cow tongues and meat joints in pickling brine. My job was to place a paddle into the brine and stir the contents, several times a day. When he needed a large beef joint or tongue for dinner he would remove it from the barrel.

My father told me about one of the tasks that he and his brothers were given when they stayed at their grandfather's farm. There was a cow tail pump on the roadside at the bottom of the very steep and winding road that levelled out on the approach to the 'big house' where my great aunt lived.

The distance from the farm to this pump was about one mile. The downhill journey, to the cow tail pump, was easy; they happily manoeuvred the large empty barrel, which was mounted on a two-wheeled cart. Once the barrel was filled with drinking water the real work began. The journey uphill to the farm was devoid of humour. However, they had two bricks to use as brakes, which they employed behind the cartwheels when a short break was required.

A donkey was available for this task, but my great grandfather probably thought that by taking the donkey out of the equation he had made work for idle hands.

I always looked forward to my visits down south and still do. My paternal family is spread throughout the four provinces of Ireland: Ulster, Munster, Leinster, and Connacht.

I had family in the Garda Síochána and, when we visited each other, we swapped stories about our lives fighting crime. My great uncle told me a story about his cousin who had been in the Lancers, an Irish cavalry unit, when they were ordered, by the British government, to march north and quell an uprising. The battalion, based at the Curragh Camp, in County Kildare, refused to go. At this time, the Curragh was the main base for the British Army in Ireland. This incident became known as the Curragh Mutiny. You should look it up. It is an informative read.

There is a long military and policing tradition in my family history, which is maintained to this day. This family service stretches back to the Peninsular Wars, the Battle of Waterloo, the second Boer War, both World Wars, the Royal Irish Constabulary, the Garda Síochána, the Royal Ulster Constabulary and the Police Service of Northern Ireland.

I made numerous visits to my family in southern Ireland during my time as a police officer. In those days, the fewer people that knew of my border crossings the better. Prior to one such visit I received a phone call from a family member asking me if I would be interested in taking part in a charity event. As the event was to raise money for cancer research, I accepted.

During this time, poker events were often used as a source to raise money for charity and other projects. The entry fee was ten punts (since that time, the euro has replaced the punt as the currency of Ireland).

There were six players per table and each game had a time limit; whoever had the most play money on each table when time was called moved to the next table, forming a table of six winners. This process continued until the final table of six players was reached. The game was seven card stud poker, with the winner taking all, which on that occasion was two hundred punts.

It was only when I arrived at the venue that I became aware of the club's name. It was a Wolfe Tone Club. Some of you may not be aware who Wolfe Tone was. He was the founder of a group known as the United Irishmen, who fought for Irish independence from British rule.

I was playing well, and, on the penultimate hand, I had two jacks showing and two buried, in other words poker jacks. I went all in, and the rest was history. I won the two hundred punts, and I gave ten punts to the player on my right, which covered his original stake.

This gesture was met with loud distain and vulgarity from the other four players. They remained ten punts down. They had been obnoxious the entire game. If only they knew what I did for a living. So why should I have worried about what they thought? Members of my family were present at the event, and they knew the organisers. The location for the event was the only premises big enough and available at the time.

You can see my dilemma; things could have mushroomed into something undesirable. I enjoyed the night despite the connotations of the location and the lies I had to tell to maintain my anonymity. It was like being undercover. I shared my winnings with my family, and we had a laugh on the return journey back to Wicklow.

I was amid racehorse country during some of my visits to counties Louth and Kildare. It was during one such visit that

I got the offer to have a ride on a racehorse. The only time that I had sat on the back of a four-legged animal was on a trip to the beach, where my parents paid for me to ride on a leisurely moving donkey. So here I was moving up from a donkey to a thoroughbred.

It was like moving from a 50cc motorcycle to a superbike.

Picture the scene, the rural equine idyll. There were people mucking out, horses were being led around, and others were riding out. Standing beside this horse I thought that I had accepted the offer too quickly. However, like most eighteen-year-olds I was full of vigour or some less respectable teenage equivalent. It was too late to back out. I had an audience who needed me to provide the entertainment.

Having donned the headgear, I was given a leg up into the saddle, while the horse was being held steady by a young lady. The first thing that came to my attention was the distance between me and the ground. I tried to remain cool, but my insides told a different story. The young lady led the horse around for a few minutes before leading it into a grassy paddock. I could feel the power below me and then she let go.

The horse stood still, patient, and serene; as instructed, I gently tapped my heels and the pace quickened, slightly.

Well, that was fast enough for me; I was enjoying myself as the horse walked around the paddock. This animal was well schooled and knew what to do. I was still enjoying myself when the horse suddenly started to pick up the pace for a short distance, then stopped all too suddenly. I was tossed out of the saddle, over the horse's head and onto the ground. It was all over in the blink of an eye. Entertainment provided.

I lay still on the ground for a moment and then moved very slowly to make sure that all was normal; it was. My family laughed as I slowly picked myself up. I was stiff for about two weeks, and I have never been on any breed of horse since. Maybe the horse knew that I was from Northern Ireland.

If you ever get a chance to visit County Kildare stay in Kildare village and visit the National Stud, which is nearby. Many famous horses have grazed its pastures.

I still visit my family in southern Ireland but not as often. I usually call them or attend family funerals, as the family circle of my peers diminishes. I miss those family days when we all mixed under one sky and where the Irish border, at least for my family, did not exist and still does not.

So, there you have it, my Irish roots. I am proud to look upon myself as having dual nationality, British and Northern Irish.

However, for the purposes of historical accuracy I should point out that my DNA makes me more than fifty percent Scottish. I am what I am, you might say, and it is what it is.

# End Note.

As my book writing journey ends, and before you place my book on the shelf, please let me share some final thoughts.

I must pay tribute to my three civilian partners, fellow experts, photographers and mappers, who attended scenes that I had examined. They saw what I saw, and I am in no doubt that this left them with lasting memories.

The photographer views the images, captures the images, processes the images, and finally compiles the images to form an album of their work. Giving evidence in court brings the photographer face to face with their work yet again.

I wonder how many of these experts suffer from PTSD and what if anything has been done to help them cope. Does anyone care? I do.

Even today, despite relative peace, the shackles of our turbulent past remain. In general, we have not moved forward as one community. There are too many open wounds festering away and feeding an underbelly of hatred and resent, with the carousel of rhetoric in full flow. I carry a graveyard in my mind, where my demons are buried. Where do you store your demons?

We will never move forward until those wielding the political swords end their wish to unite the island of Ireland under one flag. I have a simple solution, which may be too simple for some. Let us call ourselves Northern Irish, remain part of the UK and design our own all-inclusive flag.

In the spirit of that fictional army comedy, Private Frazer got it right when he uttered the words 'we're doomed.' Or are we?